$\mathcal{S}$tarry
NIGHTS

Starry
NIGHTS

JUDITH CLARKE

ALLEN&UNWIN

ACKNOWLEDGEMENTS
The ghost story Vera reads is 'The Case of Johnny Minney' from *Worlds Beyond:
From the Files of the Society for Psychical Research*, Weidenfeld and Nicolson, London,
1986 (page 124).

The 'spell' Vida chants for her mother is from
The Complete Book of Fortune, Bracken Books, London, 1994 (page 489).

First published in 2001

Allen & Unwin
83 Alexander Street
Crows Nest, NSW 2065
Australia
Phone: (61 2) 8425 0100
Fax: (61 2) 9906 2218
Email: info@allenandunwin.com
Web: www.allenandunwin.com

National Library of Australia
Cataloguing-in-Publication entry:

Clarke, Judith, 1943– .
Starry nights.

ISBN 1 86508 604 5

1. Ghosts – Juvenile fiction. I. Title.

A823.3

Cover and text design by Jo Hunt
Cover image by Steve Hunt, Pigs Might Fly Productions
Typeset by Midland Typesetters
Printed in Australia by McPherson's Printing Group

1 3 5 7 9 10 8 6 4 2

For Dr Nima Flora,
the very best of librarians

Chapter One

The house at the end of Hillcrest Road didn't look haunted, a two-storied house of sober grey brick with fresh white trimmings, less than two years old. A long gravel drive curved in from the road, the sloping lawns stretched to the dark edge of the reserve where true bush began: deep forest, mountains and valleys and gorges, threaded by narrow tracks and icy tumbling creeks. Mist rolled in at any season, thick milky clouds of it, and then the grey house seemed like a small ship alone on a vast ocean, calmly breasting the waves.

* * *

It was the second week in January. They'd been in their new house for almost two months and Jess still wasn't used to it. Every morning when she woke she expected to see her small room back at *Avalon*: the desk beneath the window, the red curtains Mum had made and the rug with red flowers to match, the faded pink paint on the walls. Instead, there was this new strange room, so big their old furniture looked lost in it, white walls which made the shadows sharper, the big bare windows that turned black at night because Vida had taken the curtains down.

Vida had taken the curtains down. Even to think of this made Jess feel funny and she turned her face into the pillow as if to shut out the awful memory of Vida grabbing those curtains, pulling and tugging until the hooks gave way and the flimsy white stuff tumbled in heaps onto the floor. Vida had stomped and trampled on them, hissing in a dreadful voice, 'I hate curtains! Hate them hate them hate them!' Then she'd gathered them up—her movements so fast and wild and furious that even to watch her had made Jess's chest go tight—and bundled them behind the wardrobe out of sight.

Since their mum got sick, Vida had been doing stuff like that: things you didn't expect, which made you jump; they were so sudden, sharp and scary. Made you want to tell on her. Tell *about* her anyway, only there wasn't anyone to tell, not with Mum sick and Dad so worried all the time.

There was Mrs Mack, of course. Mrs Mack looked after them while Dad was at work, and she was really kind, but she didn't know enough about their family, not yet. That's what Jess thought, anyway. Mrs Mack didn't know how different Vida had been when they'd lived in their old house; how Vida hadn't been a bit scary then, but a laughing kind of girl whom everybody liked.

Jess lifted her face from the stuffy pillow. There was light in the room now, the big window panes had filled up with palest blue and she could tell it was going to be a lovely day outside. Softly, hardly noticing she was doing it, Jess began humming her Nan's old song, the one her brother Clem sang too: 'Don't let the stars get in your eyes; don't let the moon break your heart . . .'

At once a voice snapped from the other bed, 'Don't sing **that** song!'

Vida. Vida was awake. She woke up really quickly these days. One minute she'd be sound asleep, the next she'd be sitting up, sharp-eyed, with all her thoughts in place.

'Don't sing it! Haven't I told you that?' and without waiting for her sister's reply Vida answered herself, as she did sometimes—and that was scary too—'I certainly have, I've told you and told you!'

Jess said nothing; sometimes that was best because Vida could make a fight out of anything you said. Jess wished she had a room of her own like she'd had back at *Avalon*. There was plenty of space in this new house—two empty bedrooms down the hall—but she knew Vida wouldn't like it if she moved because Vida had been the one who'd wanted to share. It was the first thing Vida had said when they'd seen this big room with the wide windows looking

3

out over the garden: 'Let's share, okay?' And Jess hadn't been able to say no, because then Vida might have thought Jess didn't like her any more.

Vida was out of bed now, springing from the covers in a single bold leap which carried her halfway across the room. She twirled round, once, twice, three times, and then stood still, hands on hips, her dark eyes fixed upon her sister's face. She was smiling but her smile was so tense and quivery Jess knew it could easily turn into something else, and she'd better be careful what she said.

'It's today,' Vida announced solemnly, and a tremor of sick apprehension slid down Jess's spine because she knew at once what Vida meant. She'd been hoping her sister might forget and now she saw how silly this hope had been. As if Vida would forget what she'd been talking about all week, ever since they'd seen the notice pinned up in the shop window last Thursday afternoon: Wednesday Seance, Evie Swann, 34 Willow Street, every week at 2pm. All Welcome.

'That was meant for us to see,' Vida had whispered as they stood in the street outside the newsagent's. She'd nudged her sister's arm. 'It was *meant*, Jess.' Her face had a queer hungry look, like a starving person who saw a loaf of bread held out to him. Worse than that, thought Jess now, because a starving person might actually get that loaf of bread, but her sister would never get what she was after. Vida wanted to call up a spirit, summon a soul back from wherever people went when they died.

These last few months Vida had started believing in all kinds of strange things she'd have laughed about when they'd lived back at *Avalon*. She'd tried every spell she could find in the dusty old books she brought home from op shops and garage sales; none of them ever worked and it was awful watching her try. Last Friday night when the moon was full Vida had run out into the garden, right down to the place where the big fir tree grew. From their window Jess had watched her sister walking round it backwards, round and round and round; and she knew when Vida stopped and looked up at the sky she was waiting for a spirit to come.

None did. Nothing happened, and when Vida came in from the garden her face had been pale as any ghost's. 'Don't look at me!' she'd shouted at Jess. 'Why are you always looking at me?' and quick as lightning she'd darted forward and pinched Jess on the arm. Jess had hated her then, a quick hot rush like pain, which had melted away the moment she'd heard Vida crying in her bed, crying so softly it was almost like breathing, except for the little catches in between. 'I think it was the wrong kind of tree,' Vida had sobbed. 'Because I did everything else right, didn't I? I had the words right, and it was a full moon, and seventeen times—I went round it seventeen times, didn't I?'

'Yes,' Jess had agreed, though she hadn't been counting and didn't really know.

'It was the tree then,' Vida had sighed. 'It said yew tree in the book, and I thought a yew tree was a fir. But it must be a special kind of fir, don't you think? And ours was the wrong kind?'

Evie Swann's seance would be like that, Jess felt it in her bones; the wrong kind of seance, not a proper one. All that stuff Vida had been telling her about—the table rising in the air and floating in front of you, knocks and rappings, voices, ghostly fingers plucking at your hair—they weren't going to happen at 34 Willow Street, and then Vida would be disappointed all over again. When Vida was disappointed she got angry and then Jess felt guilty, as if she was to blame. Jess didn't want to go to that seance.

Vida saw the reluctance in her face. 'You promised! You said you'd come! It needs the two of us! Two's stronger than one, especially when it's sisters!' She was shouting now, her hands clenched at her sides, and the black part of her eyes had grown so big you could hardly see the brown. Jess gave in, because Vida might start crying, she might do anything.

'It's okay, Vee,' she said quickly. 'I'll come with you.'

Chapter Two

Spells weren't the only things Vida found in her dusty old magic books. There were lots of rules as well, scratchy fussy little rules—like how you had to put your left shoe on before your right, otherwise you'd bring bad luck.

'Did you?' demanded Vida when they were almost ready to catch the bus into town. 'Did you put your left shoe on first?' Jess couldn't remember so Vida made her take both shoes off and put them on again, left one first. She made her change her t-shirt too. 'You can't go wearing green,' she said.

'Why can't I?'

'Don't you know anything? Green's the fairies' colour; they don't like humans wearing it. They'll curse you if you do, Jess.'

Vida's face was dead serious, but Jess could hardly believe what she was hearing: did Vida believe in fairies now? What would her sister's best friend Katie think? She'd think Vida had gone crazy for sure.

'Fairies?' she echoed uncertainly.

'Oh, not those kind of fairies!' Vida laughed. 'Not those cute little ones in picture books with wings and pretty party frocks.' Her eyes gleamed darkly from beneath long smoky lashes. 'I'm talking about the Little People.'

Jess didn't ask who they were. That was the trouble with Vida's spooky ideas; you didn't really believe them, yet somehow their spookiness crept into your mind. She could imagine those Little People all too clearly: they'd be like tiny adults with sour disapproving faces, so small you couldn't see them and know that they were there. They'd see you though; watching from their secret places, spying, waiting for you to do some little harmless thing you didn't know was wrong, waiting to catch you out.

Vida held up a red t-shirt. 'Here, this'll do. And hurry up, don't take so long about everything or you'll make us miss the bus!'

As if it was all her fault, brooded Jess, dragging the tight neck of the t-shirt painfully over her long fair hair. As if it was!

She'd tell Dr Snow about Vida, Jess decided as the old bus trundled down Hillcrest Road towards the town. She'd tell him the minute he got back from holidays and their appointments started up again. Dr Snow was their counsellor, a small grey man with a pointed beard and big white teeth that flashed out unexpectedly when he smiled. They saw him every week at his office in the big hospital where their mum had stayed when she first got sick. They talked to him together for half an hour, and after that she and Vida each had fifteen minutes on their own. That's when she'd tell him about those sharp scary things Vida did, and all the silly scratchy rules, and how she wanted to call a spirit back.

'Why?' Dr Snow would ask her. 'Why do you think she wants to do that, Jess?' Jess shifted uncomfortably on the sticky plastic seat; yes, he'd ask her that for sure. And she didn't know the answer, because Vida had changed so much Jess could no longer figure out her sister's thoughts.

She could guess at them: she could think up reasons why Vida might want to call a spirit, she could even guess what kind of spirit it might be—but that was too frightening to even start to think about. 'I don't know,' she heard herself saying to Dr Snow, and then he'd steeple his hands together and look at her over his fingertips, and 'I don't know,' she'd say again.

And it was true, she didn't know lots of things: like how long it would be before their mum got better, or whether they'd ever be happy again like they used to be when they lived at *Avalon*.

Back in their old house Jess had never really had to think things out, Mum was always there to answer questions, and

Dad, and Clem. Even Vida, because Vida was four years older, fourteen while Jess was only ten. Jess had gone to school and done her homework and played with her friends, that was all. Life had been easy back then; now she felt she hadn't learned anything that really mattered.

And sometimes, even though Dad said Dr Snow was the best psychologist in the city and a very famous man, Jess thought there were things he didn't know either. 'Time heals all wounds,' he'd said to them once, his voice so soft and thoughtful he could have been talking to himself. It had seemed such a cruel thing to say, though Jess knew he hadn't meant to be unkind. Vida had been really angry with him. 'No, it doesn't!' she'd shouted. 'You're wrong! It doesn't!'

Jess rested her forehead against the dusty window; outside the lonely bush crowded close against the road. It was three kilometres from their new house to the little town of Springdale, and the small green cottage at the bottom of the hill was the only house between. You never saw anyone walking on that road except for weekend hikers and the picnickers who drove up to the forest tracks above their house. On weekdays you hardly ever saw a car. At night a great blackness descended; there were no lights anywhere except for theirs, and the stars that seemed huge in the vast unfathomable sky. And when you walked out onto the terrace, no matter how hard you listened, there was never a single human sound. Jess sighed. It was all so different from the busy seaside suburb where they used to live.

'Company, that's what the pair of you need,' Mrs Mack was always telling them. 'People your own age. It's a pity my sister's family aren't coming up this summer; you'd have got on really well with the twins—they're fourteen, your age, Vida.'

Vida always wrinkled her nose when Mrs Mack talked about the twins. 'I like being on my own,' she'd say, and then Mrs Mack would sigh and shake her head. 'Everyone needs friends, lovie. But things will be better when school starts again, they're a friendly crowd at Saint Ursula's.'

'Friendly crowd of idiots,' Vida had hissed beneath her breath.

Through the window Jess saw the bus had reached the outskirts of Springdale: the Caltex service station, the Blue Hills motel, the farm with the roadside stall where fruit and vegetables were sold. Then came the bit Jess didn't like: the long stretch of road where the big trees arched across, shutting out the sky. She closed her eyes but she could still feel that cold greenish gloom pouring in through the windows, as if the bus and everyone in it had fallen down beneath the sea.

The old house called *Avalon* had been on the very edge of the bay. On sunny days shimmery water shadows danced on the walls and the sea's gentle voice had lulled them to sleep every night. Jess had loved the sea back then; now even the memory of its soft shushing sound made her think of drowning. She couldn't *stop* thinking about it; how

11

terrible it would be, how cold and aching, how you'd go down and then come up again, throat and lungs burning, your whole body screaming for air. How you might glimpse the sky and the lights of houses in the distance—and then go down again.

Dr Snow had told Jess she needed to push that drowning thought away. 'Imagine a big white tablecloth,' he'd said. 'You take it by the edges, Jess, and spread it out, then you bundle it round the bad thought and—' here Dr Snow would fling his arms out wide and his white teeth would flash inside his beard— 'and toss the whole thing away!'

Vida said that was stupid because you couldn't throw thoughts away. And she might be right because it had never worked for Jess. She could imagine the tablecloth, and grasping it by the edges, but she could never manage to wrap it round. What shape was a thought? How big or small? Her bundle never seemed to do up right and when she threw, it opened up and the drowning thought came tumbling back into her head.

The trees along the road went on for ages. Jess screwed her eyes up tighter but she could still feel that cold green gloom, and the poem she'd learned in Mrs Finch's class came creeping into her mind.

> *Full fathom five thy father lies;*
> *Of his bones are coral made;*
> *Those are pearls that were his eyes;*

Jess shivered. Dad was safe, she knew that, he wasn't lying at the bottom of the sea with coral bones and pearls for eyes. He was in his office in the city, sitting in the big chair beside his desk, the phone close to his hand, the phone she knew he'd always pick up on the very first ring in case something had happened to Mum, or in case one of them became so frightened they needed him to come home right away.

Chapter Three

You could see at once that Clem was Jess and Vida's brother. He looked like them in lots of little ways. He had Vida's dark brown eyes and thick black hair and his smile was very like Jess's: a long slow one that made you want to smile right back at him.

'My sisters have gone to a seance, would you believe?' he told his new friend Amy. They were sitting in the grassy hollow that had become their special place, right at the top of the garden where the lawn met the dark trees of the forest reserve.

'A seance?' echoed Amy doubtfully.

'You know, where everyone sits round a table and they call spirits up—or try to, anyway. It's Vee's idea—she's into all that sort of stuff.' Clem's broad forehead creased as he thought of his sister's sharp white face, that weird hungry look you sometimes saw in her eyes. 'And it's not doing her any good. I wish she'd give it away but she won't listen to me. She gets cranky if I say a word to her these days.'

'That's because . . .' began Amy, and then stopped as if she was too shy to go on with what she had to say.

Clem finished the sentence for her. 'Because she's worried about Mum.' He gazed across the lawn towards the house, catching a sudden flicker of movement at the window of his mother's room. It wouldn't be her, he knew that. Mum wouldn't go near the window; she wasn't inter-ested in anything. She'd never really seen the garden of their new house; she'd been drugged to the eyeballs when they'd brought her home from hospital. She'd never come downstairs again, never been anywhere except for that room and the small bathroom which led off it. She ate little bits of the meals they brought her, wandered in to take her shower, then she'd go back to bed again. She didn't want the radio or the television; sometimes she'd pick up a book from the bedside table, turn a few pages listlessly, and then put it down again.

The movement at the window would be Mrs Mack, clearing Mum's lunch tray away and trying hard to have a chat. Mum wouldn't say a word, and that was the worst thing of all. She never spoke to any of them. They had to keep on trying, Dad told them, keep on talking as though nothing was the matter, like you did with people lying in a coma.

Mum wasn't in a coma though.

15

'When you've never actually met anyone who's had a breakdown,' Clem said, 'you haven't a clue what it means. You've got this silly picture in your head like something from a horror movie: a person screaming, throwing themselves about, sort of . . . foaming. Noisy, you think, but it's not like that at all.'

'I know,' said Amy.

'It's quiet,' said Clem. 'A breakdown is quiet.'

Dead quiet, he thought, the way Mum just lay on that bed, day in, day out. She was a teacher, and teachers had breakdowns, everyone knew that, like poor old Crocker at his school. Only he'd never have figured Mum was the type. She wasn't a bit like poor old Twitchy Crocker, she'd always been so strong and confident, that's what they'd all thought. And they'd got it wrong somehow.

'We should have seen it coming,' he said.

'Oh no.' Amy shook her head.

'We should have. She was always worrying about those kids she taught. Some of them, anyway. The hopeless cases. She went on and on about them all the time, we should have realised—' Clem broke off, catching the whiny note in his voice. He shouldn't whinge on so much about his family, it wasn't fair to dump all his troubles on Amy, even though she always listened and didn't seem to mind. 'Sorry,' he mumbled.

His mother's window was blank and still again now. Mrs Mack had given up trying to have a conversation with someone who never said a word. She'd smooth the doona and plump the pillows, stroke the hair back from Mum's forehead, pick up the tray and go downstairs again, treading softly through their quiet house. It broke your heart to think about it.

'It mightn't be what you think.' Amy spoke the words so abruptly he turned to her in surprise.

'How do you mean?'

'Sarah. Your mum.'

Clem was puzzled. He couldn't remember telling Amy his mum's first name.

'There might be another reason why she's sick,' Amy went on hesitantly. 'It mightn't have been because of her work—'

'Another reason?'

Amy's hands twisted nervously in her lap. 'It could be because you're *here*. It's not good for her, Clem. She can't start getting better while you're here.'

'Dad thought it was best if we moved to a new place.'

Amy looked down at her hands. He hadn't understood what she'd meant, and that was her fault, because she never came right out and said it to him straight. Perhaps he wouldn't believe her if she did, because what she had to tell him might sound unbelievable. She took a deep breath. 'Clem, there's something I need to tell you.'

'About Mum?' But how could it be? he wondered. Amy had never met his mum; she'd never met any of them except for him. She was too shy to come into their house.

'No, it's—' Amy faltered again.

Clem waited. He'd been half expecting something like this. In all the weeks he'd known her, Amy had never once talked about herself. There was some kind of mystery there. She'd never even explained what she was doing wandering in their garden on the day they'd first moved in.

'Yes?' he said gently, hoping to encourage her, but now she ducked her head and her eyes were hidden from him by the wide brim of her hat. It was a hat like his mum had worn when she'd been a kid at school, a panama of soft cream straw with a bright blue velvet band.

Clem thought Amy's face was beautiful, but there was a nagging familiarity about her features which bothered him because he couldn't quite place it; he was sure he'd never met a girl who looked like her.

'Amy?' he prompted.

Amy plucked nervously at the soft blue fabric of her skirt. She'd come here because she'd made a promise to his mum, a very long time ago.

Sarah had been her very best friend at school; they'd promised they'd always watch out for each other. Sarah needed her now, and so did Clem. She had to tell him, only she didn't know how. She didn't have the courage; she'd always been hopeless at telling people things they wouldn't want to hear. That time at school before Sarah came, when awful Melanie James had asked, 'Do you want to be best friends?' and Amy had said 'yes' because she was scared of saying 'no' . . .

And what she had to tell Clem was so much worse. Amy couldn't even frame the words, she shrank from them, defeated. 'I'm hopeless,' she whispered. 'Hopeless.'

Clem laughed. "Course you're not,' he said. His laugh was such a warm easy sound it made Amy feel sad. He was so at home here; he had no inkling of what had happened. Or did he? Because sometimes Amy thought she glimpsed a sudden flicker of panic in his eyes. It vanished so quickly she could never be quite sure.

Clem reached out, snatching up the long thick braid that reached almost to her waist. It was the first time he'd ever touched her and the feeling of that warm soft plait between his fingers sent a small wave of dizziness running through him like shock. He tugged it gently, a faint blush rising to his cheeks. 'Your hair's the same colour as Jess's,' he said awkwardly.

'Jess looks like your mum when she was young.'

'How do you know?'

Now it was Amy's turn to blush. 'Oh, I just guessed.'

Later, after Clem had gone to sit with his mother, Amy came back to the grassy hollow and sat with her arms clasped round her knees, gazing at the house. She thought of Sarah and Clem, and then her thoughts turned suddenly to the little girl called Jess. Perhaps it was the resemblance, but Amy felt close to Jess, as she'd once been close to Sarah. For a moment she pictured herself walking with Jess along a sunny street, talking, laughing . . .

Amy drew her thoughts back sharply. No, of course she couldn't talk to Jess; Jess would be frightened. Clem was the only person she could talk to, in this place.

Chapter Four

Vida stood on the pavement outside Evie Swann's front gate and stared at the house in disbelief. She'd expected something so very different: a tall gloomy mansion perhaps, with ivy-covered walls, or an old wooden cottage half hidden in a mysterious garden of tangled vines and ancient twisty trees.

There was nothing at all mysterious about 34 Willow Street. It was the most ordinary kind of house: a modern brick veneer with double garage, neat lawns and tidy flowerbeds, a homemade letterbox carved in the shape of a swan. There was an air of great cheerfulness about the place.

'Oh,' sighed Vida.

'What's the matter?' asked Jess.

'It's the wrong kind of place,' said Vida. 'Nothing could happen here.'

'Want to go home then?' Jess couldn't keep the eagerness from her voice.

'No!' Vida glared at her sister, thrust the gate open and marched up the path to the porch. She'd come all this way and she wasn't giving up now, not even when the front door opened and a big jolly lady in a tracksuit beamed at them and cried, 'Why, you're the new kiddies from the house in Hillcrest Road, aren't you?'

And all the other ladies gathered round the big table in Evie Swann's front room seemed to know them too. Springdale was that sort of little town, thought Vida. A place where everyone knew everyone and new arrivals were a big event. It would be like this when they started school: all the kids would know about them before they set foot inside the gates. They'd know about Mum and everything . . .

'You girls come and sit next to me!' A small bright-eyed lady grasped Vida's hand. 'I'm Mary Tully, and that's Rose Poole over there, and Elaine Geratty—and Evie, of course!'

Evie Swann beamed at them again, her broad plain face as cheerful as her house. 'Lovely to see new faces!'

'And such young faces!' added Mary Tully delightedly.

Evie Swann's tracksuit was a vivid shade of green. Green! Vida scowled. No one who knew anything at all about the supernatural would ever conduct a seance dressed in green! You only had to look around the room to see Evie Swann didn't have a clue. Sunlight poured in through the open window, and all the noises from the street: the hum of a mower, a car going by, kids yelling somewhere down the road. Seances had to be held in quiet darkened rooms! The door to the kitchen stood open and through it Vida glimpsed plates of cakes and sandwiches, cups and saucers ready for afternoon tea. That's all they've come for, she thought scornfully.

'Shall we begin?' said Evie Swann softly, and round the table everyone took hands.

Almost at once the sound of the postman's motorbike came through the open window, chugging slowly along the footpath outside. 'A ghostly messenger,' old Elaine Geratty whispered, and a wave of laughter rippled round the table.

Vida felt like crying. She'd had such hopes for this seance, she needed so much to believe that spirits could come back—and all it was going to be was a bunch of old ladies having afternoon tea.

'Are you all right, dear?' whispered Mary Tully, and for a second, the kindness in the old lady's voice made Vida want to tell her what she'd never told a single soul: how she wanted to call a spirit back because it was the only way she could say sorry for the terrible thing she'd done that night at *Avalon*.

'I . . .' she began, but Mary Tully's next words drove the secret down again, like a dull heavy stone settling back into Vida's heart.

'It's all right lovie, nothing's going to happen. It's not a spooky seance, like those ones you see in films. No ghosts

23

or funny voices, and Evie's head won't spin round on her neck, will it, Evie?'

Evie Swann smiled broadly. 'Not if I can help it.'

'It's memories, mostly,' Mary Tully went on. 'We sit here and think about the past, old places we've known, and people—'

Vida felt her sister's hand tighten in her own. They didn't want memories; they had too many. Memories wasn't why Vida had come.

'Sad things, sometimes,' said Evie Swann. 'But happy ones too.'

'I remembered my little sister Meggsie's face last week,' Rose Poole broke in. 'The way she looked when she was young. I'd completely forgotten those little freckles on her nose.'

'It's amazing what comes back to you,' said Elaine Geratty. 'I remembered the bathroom in my gran's house—hadn't thought of it in years. The green paint on that old tub! The way it used to stick to your bum!'

They laughed again, and a dry ache burned in Vida's throat. Couldn't they be serious about anything? And they were all so old, she thought, glancing around the table at those laughing faces. They had grey hair and funny brown teeth and frail wrinkly necks that barely held their heads up straight. Any single one of them could die before next week; fall down from a heart attack, go out shopping in the rain and catch pneumonia like their own Nan had done, be driven off to hospital and never come home again.

So didn't they want to know what happened then? Get some kind of clue at least, the tiniest little hint, about where people went when they died? That they went *somewhere*, that they were still *them*, the people they'd been when they'd closed their eyes. Didn't they?

The room had grown quiet now, but Vida was so wrapped up in her angry thoughts she noticed nothing more until she heard Mary Tully's voice asking, 'Are you all right, dear?'

Vida tensed in her chair. Why did she have to keep on asking her that? Why couldn't she leave her alone?

But when she looked up Vida saw it was Evie Swann her neighbour was concerned about. Evie Swann had gone very, very pale. 'Oh,' she was whispering. 'Oh.'

'Evie?'

Chairs scraped as the old ladies rose from the table and clustered round their friend, patting her back and shoulders, stroking her curly white hair. 'Evie love, what's wrong?'

Evie Swann fluttered a plump hand against her chest. 'I thought I heard a voice.'

Everyone went quiet.

'A voice?'

Vida gazed sternly across the table. She was almost certain Evie Swann was pretending, because if there'd been a voice it would have been for her. She'd have heard it too.

'What kind of voice?' she asked, so sharply that Jess flinched and Evie Swann's friends turned to stare.

'What kind?' Evie Swann considered the question, closing her eyes for a long moment, gathering her thoughts. 'A young girl's voice,' she replied at last, and then Vida knew for sure she was lying because the voice she longed to hear would never have been a girl's.

Rose Poole nodded briskly towards the window. 'That would have been young Susan from next door, Evie. I saw her out in her front yard when I came up your path.'

'Oh yes, Susan—' Mrs Swann didn't sound very sure.

'But what did she say?' Elaine Geratty's face was alight with curiosity.

'Well, that's the funny thing—' Evie Swann kneaded at her forehead. 'I couldn't make it out.'

'The words?'

'Oh no, the words were plain enough. It was more that I couldn't understand why she'd say something like that, if she was, you know—'

'What?'

'Well, some kind of—ghost.'

Rose Poole sucked in her breath. 'A ghost! Oh, come now, Evie!'

'But say something like what, love?' pressed Elaine Geratty. 'Evie, what *did* she say?'

'She *said*,' Evie Swann brought the words out carefully, one by one. 'She said, "I'm hopeless, hopeless."'

'That would be young Susan for sure,' said Rose Poole. 'And she's certainly no ghost!'

They all laughed at that. Even Evie Swann laughed. She was looking better now, the colour flooding back into her cheeks.

Vida jumped up angrily from her chair. She couldn't bear to stay a moment longer. She knew there hadn't been any voice; Evie Swann had been pretending; they were making a joke of everything. She grabbed her sister's arm.

'Let's go.'

'But—'

'Come on,' Vida tugged Jess from her chair; everyone stared at them.

'You're not leaving, love?'

'There's afternoon tea now.'

'You'll stay for that, won't you?'

'Elaine's made her cherry sponge!'

'There's my meringues!'

'And lamingtons.' Mary Tully nudged Jess. 'You like lamingtons, don't you?'

Jess wanted to stay. 'We—'

Vida cut her short. 'We can't. We're late. Our mum will wonder where we are.' Ignoring everyone, she steered her little sister firmly to the door.

Chapter Five

Out in the street Vida kicked angrily at the ferns beside Evie Swann's front fence.

'Don't!' pleaded Jess, glancing anxiously back at the window, relieved to see no watching faces there. 'Don't, Vee.'

She'd known the seance would end like this, with Vida getting disappointed and cross and wild.

Vida glowered at her. 'You're glad it didn't work, aren't you? You're glad it wasn't a proper seance.'

'No I'm not.'

'Yes you are.' Vida kicked the ferns again.

'It was stupid in there, stupid! Silly old chooks playing games.'

'But that lady, Evie Swann—' Jess faltered, frightened by the bitter gleam in Vida's eyes.

'What about her?'

'She heard a voice, didn't she? I thought you wanted—'

'Of course she didn't hear a voice,' said Vida angrily. 'She made that up, didn't she?'

'How do you know?'

'I just do.' Vida's mouth twisted into an ugly shape. 'As if a spirit would talk to *that* old show-off! And if one did, if there *had* been a voice, then *I'd* have heard it, wouldn't I?'

'I don't know,' said Jess uneasily.

'Of course I would! Or—' Vida eyed her sister narrowly. 'You might have.'

'Me?'

'Yes, you. *Did* you hear anything?'

'No!'

'There! I knew it was only stupid old ladies fooling round.'

'They were nice,' said Jess. 'And it was mean of us to run away like that. They really wanted us to stay.'

'Oh, shut up!'

Jess shrank back from the hot dark light which seemed to pour from Vida's eyes. It wasn't fair, the seance hadn't been her idea, she hated all that kind of spooky stuff.

'It's you who wanted to go,' she protested. 'I don't want to talk to spirits. I never did.'

She didn't have to, thought Vida bitterly. Jess hadn't done anything, Jess didn't need to say sorry like she did. The stony weight of her secret pressed hard against Vida's heart, stinging tears gathered suddenly in her eyes and she turned her head quickly so her sister wouldn't see. But Jess must have noticed because her small hand, all wet and sticky like a little kid's, reached out and patted Vida's arm.

'Get off!' Vida flicked it away.

'Vee? What's the matter, Vee? Why—' Jess's voice quivered, 'why do you want to talk to spirits anyway? Why do you? Is it because . . .'

'Oh, leave me alone!' Hitching her bag up on her shoulder, Vida turned and rushed off down the street.

'Vee! Wait for me!'

Vida didn't even look round. She ran on blindly towards the shopping centre, long skirt flapping, bag bumping against her bony shoulderblades. Trees and houses and telegraph poles blurred before her eyes. No one knew what she had done back there at home, in that dear lovely house called *Avalon*, no one knew how she was to blame for Mum being sick, for everything. *What you did*, her small black pointy boots beat out on the pavement as she flew along, *What you did what you did what you did.*

Chapter Six

Springdale was such a small place you couldn't get lost in it, that's what their dad always said, but Jess couldn't find Vida anywhere. She wasn't at the bus stop or in the small red-brick library beside the park, she wasn't in the post office or the supermarket—Jess hurried up the main street again, peering through shop doors. Outside the chemist's she stopped and looked back.

She didn't know what made her do this. Had she heard a sound? A sound so very soft it might have been a mouth opening quietly in the air? The sense of someone right behind her, standing very still? Vida playing tricks like she sometimes did? There was no one there, yet as Jess hurried on the same feeling crept over her again, only now it was as if someone was walking beside her, quietly keeping step. She glanced sideways, quickly. At first she thought there was nothing; then she looked downwards and saw a wavy strip of shimmering blue floating in the air above the pavement, like someone's lost hair-ribbon drifting in the breeze.

But there was no breeze today and it couldn't be a hair-ribbon because when Jess stopped walking it stopped too and hovered in the air beside her, very still. The tiny hairs prickled at the back of her neck—it was some kind of *thing*—she jumped back and it jumped after her, brushing the bare skin of her knee. Its touch felt soft and cool, like cloth. Jess began to run but the blue thing kept pace, bouncing and twirling beside her.

The blood pounded in Jess's ears but everything else had gone strangely silent. She couldn't hear the sounds of the street any more; voices and footsteps, the cars passing by on the road. She ran faster and it went faster too, it wouldn't go away. 'Oh please,' Jess whispered, begging. 'Please, please go away.'

It did as she asked. As if it could hear her, the blue thing folded itself away inside the air, neatly and quietly, like a tongue sliding back inside a mouth. And at once the ordinary sounds of the street came rushing back: traffic and people, a mum scolding her little kid outside the super-market, 'Lissie, I can't be bothered with that now!'

Jess stared dazedly into the window of the hardware store: cans of paint, rollers and brushes, they hardly made sense any more. She was trembling all over. Had she really seen that? Had she really seen a thing coming out of the air? Coming out and then sliding back again, so horribly it made a cold little wave run down her spine?

She couldn't have, she must have imagined it, or made it up, like Vida said Evie Swann had made up the voice she'd heard.

Except Jess didn't believe Evie Swann *had* made that voice up—people who made up stuff didn't look so pale and scared. Evie Swann *had* heard a voice. A frightening thought seized Jess: could that funny blue thing have followed her from Willow Street? Old Mary Tully had said it wasn't a proper seance, and Vida thought so too, but could something have still got through? Jess shuddered, remembering the cool soft feel of it against her leg. She stooped and brushed the place where it had touched; the warm rough skin of her knee was just the same as ever.

It was her feet that had gone funny, damp and very cold, as if the blue thing had somehow frozen them. She looked down and found she was standing in a pool of muddy water. The dusty pavement had been hosed down, there were puddles all along the street. A green car passed by on the road and its colour rippled in the water, flashed up into her eyes.

Could that be what she'd seen? Had a blue car driven past her, its bright colour dazzling from those puddles on the ground? Had that cool soft touch she'd felt only been drops of water sprayed from her running feet? It could have been, thought Jess hopefully, it could have been.

Only the way the thing had vanished . . . Jess put out her hand to the place where she'd seen it go, half expecting to feel a long scaly seam stitched into the air. There was nothing.

Light fingers touched her shoulder. Jess jumped.

'Scared you!'

It was only Vida.

'Oh, Vee!' Jess flung her arms round her sister, hugging her tight.

'Hey, what's the matter?'

Once Jess used to tell her sister every little thing that bothered her, especially when she felt scared, and Vida would always explain away her fears. Back then Vida would have agreed that what Jess had seen was only the reflection of a passing car.

Now Vida's head was so full of spooky stuff Jess knew she'd say that strange blue thing was ghostly, and had followed her from Willow Street. 'It would have been looking for *me*,' Vida would explain. 'That's why it followed you, Jess. Because you were my sister and it knew you'd come to me.'

You couldn't really talk to Vida any more.

'Hey, what's up?'

'Nothing,' Jess mumbled. 'It was just . . . I couldn't find you.'

'Well, I'm here now.' Vida smiled and Jess noticed she looked completely different from the angry girl who'd run away down Willow Street. Something had happened, Jess thought, something Vida thought was good. Her eyes shone with excitement, she hugged a flat brown parcel close against her chest. 'Guess what I found in the op shop!'

So that's where she'd been. Jess eyed the parcel; the thick brown paper was crumpled and used. Another dusty old book of spells, that's what it would be, and Vida had forgotten her disappointment with the seance because she thought one of those spells would help her call a spirit back. It wouldn't, of course, and then Jess would wake up to find her sister crying in the night.

'A book?'

'No!' Vida laughed. 'It's better than that, much, much better!' She grabbed Jess by the arm. 'Come on, let's go down to the bus stop and I'll show you!'

Chapter Seven

There would be rules for undoing knots, Jess thought as she watched Vida tearing at the string around her parcel, some of those fussy little rules to keep bad luck away, only Vida was so excited she'd forgotten all about them.

The knot wouldn't budge. As Vida turned the parcel on its side to get a better grip, a strange little skirring noise came from inside the brown wrapping, like tiny claws scrabbling to get out.

'There!' Vida pulled the string away and folded back the paper. Jess saw a round wooden board with a hole at the top where a pencil was fixed through. The tiny wheels beneath it would have made the skirring sound.

'What is it?'

'A planchette.'

Jess stared at the round wooden board on her sister's lap. She didn't know what a planchette was but she didn't like the look of it; she'd never seen wood that colour, the gleaming dangerous yellow of a big cat's eye.

'What's a planchette?'

'You really don't know anything, do you? A planchette's for spirit writing—' Vida touched the pencil gently with a fingertip, 'for getting messages, and . . . and giving them.'

'How?'

'You lay it on a sheet of paper, on a table or something, and then you rest your hand on it.' Vida placed hers flat on the board, it made a little slapping sound. 'And *your* hand too, of course, you put yours on top of mine, so it's both of us, see? And then it moves across the paper on these little wheels and the pencil writes the messages.'

Jess frowned. 'Does it?'

'Oh yes!' For once Vida didn't seem to notice the doubt in her sister's voice. Her eyes glowed. 'Oh Jessie, I was so lucky, you know. I nearly didn't see it. It was right at the back of the shop under a pile of old tablecloths; I almost walked right by. And then something made me stop and I saw the edge of it. Oh Jess, what if I'd walked right past and missed it? Except I don't think I would have, I think it was meant for me to find . . .'

Jess hated it when Vida talked like this—so fast it was a kind of babble, and her eyes didn't look at you. Like you weren't really there and she was chattering away to herself.

'We'll set it up on that big table in the kitchen, really

late, when Mrs Mack's gone home and everyone's asleep, and then . . .'

'I don't want to,' whispered Jess. The gleaming yellow colour of the board gave her the same scary feeling the blue thing did; you felt it had come from somewhere else, a place outside the world.

'Why don't you want to? It won't work with only one of us, it needs us both, it needs *sisters*.'

'I don't like it.'

Vida's voice took on the whiny note that always came before the bullying. 'I do stuff for you. I help you with your homework, I let you hang around with me and my friends, even though you're only a kid.'

'You should answer Katie's letters.'

There were three of them lying on the table in the hall; Jess saw them every time she walked past, Katie's familiar writing on the envelopes. Vida hadn't even opened them, and Katie was her very best friend.

'I'll get round to it,' Vida said stiffly and then changed the subject, like she always did when Katie's name was mentioned. 'Look, I loan you pocket money when yours runs out, don't I? And I talked Dad into letting you buy that black cossie he said was way too old for you.'

'That's different.'

'How?'

Jess couldn't explain. This stuff Vida was talking about—homework and pocket money, Katie, the cossie—it was ordinary. The planchette was different, creepy, like the thing that had followed her in the street, bouncing and twirling, lifting and falling . . .

Like the hem of someone's skirt, Jess thought suddenly. That's what it had looked like, as if an invisible girl had been running along beside her, and the only piece you could see was the very bottom of her skirt. It could even be that girl whose voice Evie Swann had heard . . .

Jess glanced sideways at the yellow board on Vida's lap. What if it did work? What if there *was* some kind of ghost, and the planchette brought her closer, let more of her get though?

'How is it different?' repeated Vida.

'It just is.'

Vida's fingers clenched. Jess edged away along the seat, and when Vida saw this a sudden shamed expression crossed her face. 'Don't be scared of me, Jess,' she whispered. 'Please don't be.'

'I'm not.'

'Look, I'm sorry I got mad with you the other night, I'm sorry I—' Vida flushed— 'pinched you. I didn't mean to, honest. I sort of can't help it, Jess. I get all worked up, here.' She laid a hand against her chest. 'It's like something just rushes in. I'm sorry, okay?'

Jess didn't know what to say. It seemed so strange and sad and embarrassing having her big sister apologise and look ashamed. She stared down at the ground, at the torn chip packets and ice-cream wrappers scattered in front of the seat.

Pleading fingers stroked her arm. 'Okay, you know what I'm going to do? I won't pester you about it, all right? The planchette? I promise. I'll wait till you change your mind.'

'But I won't.'

'Yes you will. You'll change your mind after you've thought about it. It's silly to be scared of things you don't understand, Jess.'

'It's not that.' Jess kept her head down, avoiding Vida's eyes.

'Oh, I know you think I haven't got any patience,' Vida went on. 'You think I can't wait, but I can wait for ages, without even saying anything, you'll see. I'll put it away in the wardrobe where you won't even have to see it.'

Vida was talking really fast again, and if she kept on Jess knew she'd give in, like she'd done with the seance, like she did with everything, because she loved her sister, even though Vida scared her now.

The sun shone down gently, warming her skin and hair; it was the beautiful day promised through the wide windows when she'd woken up this morning. In the park across the road little kids were shouting, playing tiggie while their mums sat on the benches chatting. An old lady with a big black poodle walked slowly round the pond. It all looked so peaceful and ordinary but Jess knew everything had changed. A little slit had opened in the air and it could get wider . . .

'Jessie?' Vida's hand was on her arm. 'Jessie, listen to me.'

Jess lifted her eyes and saw the Hillcrest bus edging slowly round the corner. She jumped up from the seat. 'Here's the bus!' she cried, and Vida's hand dropped away.

The Hillcrest bus was old and battered, thick dust and long shallow dents along its sides, but to Jess it might have been a knight in shining armour riding nobly to her rescue. One more second and she'd have given in to Vida.

Chapter Eight

Mrs Mack had been in their room while they were out. Their new Saint Ursula's uniforms lay neatly on their beds, freshly ironed, ready to try on.

'Huh!' growled Vida, grabbing hers and flinging it onto a chair. 'School!'

But Jess couldn't wait to start at Saint Ursula's; she wasn't even scared of being new. She longed for school in the way she normally longed for holidays; she wanted hot stuffy classrooms smelling of chalk and sweat and the mouldy old orange left in someone's bag; bells jangling, rushing feet and noisy voices in the corridors, teachers shouting, 'Walk, don't run!'

School would be safe, there'd be people all round her. The air wouldn't open there.

She picked up her school-dress and held it against her chest, a drab green frock with buttons down the front,

42

a brown collar and brown bands around the sleeves. There was a dark green blazer and a summer hat which wasn't all that different from the one their mum had worn at school, a soft cream panama with a brown band and the shiny badge of their school.

Behind her the wardrobe door creaked open. 'I'm going to put it up here,' announced Vida. 'The planchette? On the top shelf, all right? Jess, are you listening to me?'

Jess dropped her school-dress on the bed and turned round. Vida stood in front of the wardrobe, the planchette in one hand. Indoors its strange yellow colour was so vivid and unnatural that Jess had to fight the urge to run away. She took a small step backwards and her sister laughed.

'It won't hurt you, stupid. It won't bite. Here!' She thrust the planchette towards Jess. 'Touch it. Go on!'

'I don't want to.'

'Oh, don't be such a scaredy!' With one of her quick sudden movements, Vida sprang forward and grabbed her sister's hand, pressing Jess's fingers against the shiny wood.

'Let me go!'

'Honestly, you're hopeless! Anyone would think you were four instead of ten.'

Jess drew in a breath. 'It feels warm.'

'That's because your fingers are cold.' Vida released her hand. 'Wood can feel warm if your fingers are cold, don't you know that?'

When Jess didn't answer she added, 'You're like a baby,

aren't you? Scared of everything. Anyway, I'm putting it away now, out of your sight.' She stood on tiptoe and slid the planchette under the folded blankets on the shelf. 'See? All gone. Baby.'

And then the teasing note dropped suddenly away. 'All gone,' she said again, and her voice was so sad it made Jess's heart ache, made her remember *Avalon* and how happy they'd been back there.

All gone.

Jess's gaze met her sister's. Vida whispered, 'I'd give anything if it worked, I'd give anything for just one single word—' her eyes drifted to the wide bare windows full of sky that made you think of heaven— 'from there.'

Jess couldn't bear it. 'You promised you wouldn't pester!' she cried out.

'I wasn't pestering!' Angry crimson flared in Vida's cheeks. 'I wasn't even talking to you! I was saying something private, to myself! Oh, I can't even be bothered with you, you're such a baby!' She flung her head back, dark hair flying, and ran towards the door, where she turned to hiss at Jess, 'Stupid little scaredy cat!'

Then there was only the sound of her black boots clattering down the stairs.

Alone in the room, Jess picked up her new school-dress from the bed and crossed to the mirror above the chest of drawers. She held the dress against her shoulders and peered into the glass. All she could see was a fuzzy dark outline and above it a blur of white face. She turned round. What had happened? When they'd come in, the room had been filled with sunlight, now it was gloomy and cold.

She went to the window. Outside big purple clouds had rolled across the sky, the garden lay in shadow and the sudden darkness felt really spooky, as if the world had gone all wrong and night was coming in the middle of the afternoon.

At *Avalon* storms had come quickly too: in a moment, the blue bay would turn to ash, the wind and waves would rise, little boats got smashed and drowned. Mrs Finch's poem came sliding back: *Full fathom five thy father lies; Of his bones are coral made . . .*

Jess shivered, she wouldn't think of drowning, she wouldn't, even though the room felt very cold and she was almost sure that she could smell the sea. The air was stretched tight as if something might burst through at any second. Lightning streaked across the sky. A clap of thunder shook the walls and then the rain began, sweeping across the garden, down the drive, hurling itself against the windows, stamping and clattering on the roof.

And just as suddenly it stopped, leaving a perfect little silence in the centre of the storm. The lashing trees, the bowing bushes, every blade of grass stood still and separate—and out there on the wide slope of the lawn Jess saw a patch of brilliant blue. It was bigger now, a different shape; the narrow strip had lengthened, become the lower

45

half of a full blue skirt which flared out and and then fell into quiet folds, as if the person wearing it had been walking over the grass, and suddenly stood still.

Was she really seeing that? Jess pressed closer to the window but she wasn't quick enough because the rain began again, a thick white sheet of it let down abruptly from the sky, hiding everything away.

Chapter Nine

'It ran after me, Mum, all along the street. And you know what I can't help thinking?'

With the dusky evening pressing close against the window of her mother's room, Jess was almost certain the frightening idea which had taken hold of her that afternoon was true.

'I think it was the girl,' she whispered to her mum. 'You know, that girl Evie Swann said she heard at the seance? It was only the edge of her skirt I saw, but I could sort of feel the rest of her, behind the air.' Jess's small hands sketched the shape of a girl: head and shoulders, slender body, those quick invisible legs that moved in time with hers, flipping the blue hem of the skirt about her knee.

'And Mum, she might have followed me here. I think I saw her in the garden when it was raining; she was just standing there.' Jess slid along the edge of the bed till she was as close to her mum as she could get. 'But it couldn't have been, could it, Mum? A ghost girl? Because there's no such things as ghosts, are there?'

Her mother's eyes were closed but Jess could tell she wasn't sleeping. Could she hear what Jess was saying? The way she never answered made you feel she wanted nothing to do with you, but Dr Snow said that was your own feeling, not Mum's. Their mum had gone deep inside herself, he told them, as people did sometimes when they got hurt or had a shock; and Jess imagined her mum—her real mum, the way she used to be—curled up small as a seed inside this quiet lady on the bed.

'No such things as ghosts, that's what you'd say, Mum, if you were better, wouldn't you? I know you would, and I know I shouldn't be silly, only—' Jess's fingers twisted at the doona cover— 'I can't help thinking, see? Vida's found this creepy board; she says it writes spirit messages. It couldn't, could it, Mum? She wants me to help her with it, but I'm scared. What if it let that ghost girl through, brought all of her? She might do something to us, Mum. I don't know what, she might—she might take one of us away. Ghosts do that sometimes, don't they? There's a story like that in one of Vida's books . . .'

Jess stopped, hearing her sister's footsteps in the hall. 'Our new school's called Saint Ursula's,' she went on in a bright high cheerful voice, 'and Mrs Mack says the girls are really friendly there.'

The light snapped on suddenly. Vida came in and stood leaning against the wall.

'Oh, stop babbling, why don't you?' she said to Jess. 'Can't you see it isn't any use? She doesn't care about stupid stuff like school. She doesn't care about anything.'

'But Dr Snow says we should tell her things.'

'He doesn't know, does he?' cried Vida. 'How can he? He hasn't got someone like Mum at home, someone who can't be bothered with him any more.'

'She *can* be bothered. I mean, she will when she gets better.'

'How do you know? How does anyone?' Vida cast a stricken glance towards the bed, her cruel secret stabbing painfully like it always did when she saw her mum. A sudden picture rose in her mind of her mother in hospital. How terrible that had been, seeing her sitting in the awful dayroom; the sick-coloured walls, the TV bolted to them, perched up high like a big square eye gleaming down on everyone.

And those people—that man who'd been hunched up in a corner banging his head against the wall, the lady with the handbag who'd kept on walking round and round . . .

Mum wasn't like them, was she? She couldn't be. But if she was, if she never got well again, Vida knew that was her fault too.

She rushed blindly at the bed, pushing Jess aside. 'Mum,'

49

she whispered hoarsely, seizing her mother's hand and squeezing it fiercely in hers.

'Oh Mum, Mum Mum Mum.'

Chapter Ten

Whenever Clem came to his mum's room, he'd sit on the chair and put one foot up on the bed, resting it on the clean crisp cover of the doona. He knew it was a childish thing to do, but he couldn't help hoping that one day Mum would see that foot and swipe it, exclaiming crossly, 'Clem, will you get that filthy sneaker off my clean bed!'

Not tonight though. Clem gazed at her sadly. No matter how long it went on he couldn't get used to her silence. She'd always been such a *talky* person. The minute she came in the door from school, before she'd even put her bag down and taken off her coat, she'd be raving on about those kids she taught, the ones in 9E, where they dumped all those hopeless cases Mum thought she could save.

Like Danny Hannan. Danny Hannan had been chucked out halfway through last year. Mum had tried to stop that happening but she hadn't had a chance. Later on she'd run into him in town; he'd been begging outside the station and when he spoke to her she'd spotted a small shiny bead in the centre of his tongue. 'I thought it was a lolly,' she'd told them. 'You know, one of those little silver cachous you put on birthday cakes? But it was a stud, right through the centre of his tongue.'

'Ugh.' Jess had shuddered.

Danny Hannan had been thin and hollow-cheeked, grey-skinned. Wasted. On drugs, probably. 'And he's just the kind of careless kid who'd use someone else's needle,' Mum had worried.

'Stupid,' Vida had said. 'He'd have to be stupid, Mum.'

Mum had got really angry then. 'It's not a question of being stupid, Vida. That's not the point. It's—'

Clem hadn't heard the rest. Mum had been all upset and he'd just strolled off to his room, and Vida and Jess had probably strolled off too—they were all so used to her raving on about kids like Danny Hannan that they never took her seriously, never noticed how things like that were really hurting her.

Background music, he thought, that's how they'd treated her. The Sound of Mum.

And now he didn't know what to do. None of them did, not even Dad. How could you bring her back? He couldn't even think what to say to her, couldn't talk naturally like Jess and Dad did, he was almost as bad as Vee.

Poor old Vee. Of all of them, she was taking it the

hardest, maybe she felt guilty too. Clem leaned his head against the back of the chair and softly, hardly aware he was doing it, began humming that old song of Nan's, the one that had lodged so firmly in his brain he'd probably be humming it when he was eighty-five. 'Don't let the stars get in your eyes; don't let the moon break your heart . . .'

Mum heard it. She must have, because her eyes flicked open and she was gazing straight at him, looking slightly puzzled, as if she'd heard his voice all right and saw him sitting there but couldn't figure out who he was.

He leaned forward and took her hand. 'It's okay Mum, it's me.'

'Clem,' she whispered. 'Clem?'

She'd said his name!

'Yeah, Clem. Remember?' He grinned at her but she only sighed and turned her eyes to the window.

'There's a great garden out there, Mum,' he said awkwardly. 'You should see it. When you're better, when you come downstairs. I'll show you.'

He suddenly thought of Amy. Mum used to tease him about girls. He'd hated it, he hadn't wanted her to know, but now he said, 'Hey Mum, guess what? I met this girl out there. In the garden, I mean. She's called Amy, and you'd like her, I bet. She's quiet, and sort of mysterious. She wears these funny old-fashioned clothes . . .'

His mother had closed her eyes again, like she was tired

53

of him or something. He knew it wasn't that, he knew he shouldn't think that way. And she'd said his name today, and looked at him. That was great. It was a start anyway.

✳ ✳ ✳

Later, Sarah opened her eyes and looked around the room. She thought she'd heard Clem humming that old song of her mum's, she thought she'd seen him sitting in the chair beside the bed. He'd talked to her, he'd held her hand.

He shouldn't be here, Sarah thought, turning her head restlessly on the pillow. He shouldn't be. But she didn't want to think about Clem, not now. She didn't want to think about any of them. She didn't want to be here in this room.

Sarah closed her eyes and drifted back to a safe and happy place. The sun shone there, and young voices clamoured and a teacher called gaily, 'Mary Nolan, pick up that paper, if you please!'

She was standing with her best friend in the upper quad at school, leaning against the railing, gazing down at the boys in the playground below. Boys—boys running, shouting, jumping, spinning round, punching and kicking things: footballs and dustbins, schoolbags, other boys. Jimmy Bowman had Martin Crawshaw on the ground, kneeling on his chest, Ian Shepherd had Jeffie Spears in a headlock, dragging him round the yard.

'It's like they can't keep still even if they want to,' remarked Sarah's friend. 'Like they've got keys in their backs underneath those filthy jumpers and someone's wound them really tight, and then let go—fizzzz!'

The boys had hoarse voices and rough spiky hair, pimples on their faces, scabs on their elbows and knees. It was weird to think how they'd get married some day. 'Even Jeffie Spears,' said Sarah.

'Jeffie Spears!'

'Some girl will think he's wonderful and fall in love with him. Imagine!'

They giggled at the very thought.

'I'll tell you something about that girl, but,' said Sarah's friend. 'That girl who falls in love with Jeffie Spears. She won't have—won't have—' The friend was laughing so much she couldn't finish. Sarah did it for her. 'That girl won't have gone to school with him, like us!'

Chapter Eleven

As she fell asleep that night, Vida heard the sharp ringing of a telephone. She knew by the way it stopped the moment she woke, and the familiar little burble in between the rings that it wasn't the telephone downstairs in the hall.

It was the nightmare telephone—the phone at *Avalon* which had rung very late that night when Mum got sick, and now kept ringing eerily in Vida's dreams. If she didn't wake quickly enough she'd hear Mum's voice too, just as she'd heard it that night, Mum's answering 'hello' all soft and nervous because it had been so very late to get a call.

There'd been a long silence after that 'hello', and Vida remembered how, as she'd lain there listening, the soft white curtains at the window of her old room had billowed out and flattened, sighed. She'd see those curtains too, sometimes, printed on the dark behind her eyes.

Vida turned in her bed and stared at the blank white

wall. What would happen if Mum didn't get better? Would she have to go back to that hospital and live there, like really crazy people did? Like that man who'd kept knocking his head against the wall? Would she get worse? Could people die of having breakdowns? *Could* they? They might, thought Vida; they might just give up and die—and if Mum did that, it would be Vida's fault too, because of what she'd done.

It had been a very small thing, so small and ordinary you'd never dream it could ruin all their lives. Vida hadn't meant to do it, how could she ever have guessed what would happen because she'd turned that little knob? She could still hear the click it had made, like the tap of a goblin's claw. But not meaning to do something didn't count. *'For want of a nail the shoe was lost,'* recited Vida silently,

> *For want of a shoe the horse was lost,*
> *For want of a horse the rider was lost,*
> *For want of a rider the battle was lost,*
> *For want of a battle the kingdom was lost.*

That's what she'd done, thought Vida miserably: she'd lost her family's kingdom and nothing would ever go right for them until she could say sorry for what she'd done. And to say sorry, to say it right and to the person it was meant for, she had to call that spirit back. She knew she had to, it was the only way.

She slipped out of bed and tiptoed to the wardrobe. She took the planchette from its shelf and carried it carefully to the desk beneath the window. There was a sheet of paper ready there, and enough moonlight to see. 'Are you there?' she whispered. 'Are you?'

The tiny wheels carried the board smoothly across the paper. In the quiet room they made a sound like the sleepy sea, shee-sha, shee-sha; but when Vida held the paper up to the silvery window, all she could make out were faint scribbles and long wavy lines. There was no message; it wasn't working. She'd known it wouldn't with only her.

It had to be the two of them, it had to be sisters to make the calling strong enough to be heard. Vida turned her head and gazed across the room towards her sister's bed. It was useless pestering her, Jess would only dig her heels in now she was scared. If she could only tell her why she needed the planchette to work, why she had to say sorry, then Jess might help. But Vida couldn't tell her, she couldn't tell anyone in the family because they might hate her then.

She placed her hand on the planchette and tried one more time. 'Are you there?' she pleaded. 'Please, please come.'

Shee-sha, shee-sha, the tiny wheels scurried across the paper. Jess heard them through her sleep and dreamed she was walking on the green foreshore back at home. The sun was shining, the bay was calm and still; she didn't seem to be scared of the sea any more.

A hand fell on her arm and its touch was soft as cloth and Jess's heart froze because she knew it was the ghost girl.

'You'll soon see more of me,' the girl whispered. 'You'll see a little bit and then another little bit until you see the whole of me, until at last you'll see my face—'

'No!' Jess wouldn't look at her, she wouldn't turn her head; the face would be a wicked goblin face, twisted up with hate and fury, like that ghost she'd read about in Vida's story, the one who'd taken the child away. Jess tried to run but her legs had gone thick and heavy, dull sullen things that wouldn't do what she wanted. She couldn't get away . . .

And then another voice entered Jess's dream, a brisk voice, comforting and cheerful. 'It's all right, dear,' promised Mrs Mack. 'Things will be better when school starts again.'

'School,' Jess murmured. 'School.'

She's dreaming about school, thought Vida scornfully as she climbed back into bed. Jess thought they'd make all these new friends when they started at Saint Ursula's, but Vida knew they wouldn't. Everyone would know about them. She and Jess would be the new kids everyone felt sorry for because terrible things had happened in their family. They'd be special cases, freaks. Kids would be nice to them, but they wouldn't be friends, not real ones, not like Katie. They'd keep their distance in case bad things happening was catching. You always felt uneasy with people you had to be sorry for.

That was why Vida hadn't opened Katie's letters, in case, on her new Christmas-present stationery, Katie was feeling sorry for her.

Chapter Twelve

Clem knelt at the window of his room, forehead pressed against the cold glass, elbows propped on the windowsill.

The stars seemed bigger here, closer to the earth, or perhaps after the storm the sky was very clear. It was one of those special starry nights he'd loved so much back home, when the dazzling sky above the bay made him brim with such excitement it seemed ridiculous to tamely go to bed. So he'd take the boat out, Dad's little boat, the *Sarah Jane*. It was his secret; Dad didn't know about those trips, or Mum, or anyone. There was no point in telling them, they'd only have fussed and they didn't need to, Clem knew the bay like the back of his hand; he'd been sailing with Dad since he was five. That secret sailing on those special starry nights was the thing he'd loved most in the world.

He missed the sea so much, the sound of it at night, the view of it through the windows of his old room at *Avalon*, like some shining mysterious country waiting for him to explore. Clem sighed, there was no sea outside this window—all he could make out was the pale sweep of lawn and the darker shapes of trees. Where the lawn sloped up to the grassy hollow the starlight seemed brighter, shimmery.

Amy's place, he thought. That's where he'd met her on the day they'd moved in; he'd been looking round the garden and there she'd been, sitting in the grassy hollow, her feet tucked neatly beneath her wide blue skirt, hands folded primly in her lap. 'Oh, it's you,' she'd said, almost as if she'd been expecting him.

He'd thought she was a neighbour at first, till he'd discovered they had no neighbours, except for the Whittakers in the green cottage at the bottom of the hill. The Whittakers were elderly, with grown-up children who lived in Adelaide, so Amy didn't come from there.

Clem drummed his fingers on the sill. It was funny how she'd never said where she came from, how she was sort of . . . just there. Mysterious, like he'd said to Mum. Her clothes were funny too: the blue tunic thing with the white blouse underneath, the hat, the thick black stockings and heavy polished shoes. A school uniform, of course, it had to be, a really old-fashioned one.

School uniform worn in the middle of January gave him a sort of clue, because it had to mean boarding school. There were boarding schools scattered through the hills;

and Amy's one must be really strict if they made her wear uniform in the holidays.

'Are you at school round here?' It was the simplest question, but he couldn't bring himself to ask it, because being left at school in January surely meant something was wrong, the kind of painful circumstances Amy mightn't want to talk about. Parents who'd dumped her while they went off overseas, perhaps. Or no parents . . . that could explain why she never talked about her family.

Poor Amy. Clem pictured her walking down empty echoing corridors, sitting at dinner opposite some grim-faced teacher who'd also been left behind. No wonder she didn't want to talk about herself, no wonder she sneaked out and came wandering here. Clem frowned. Amy never looked as if she'd been wandering; her blue tunic was always creaseless, there was never a speck of dust on those shiny shoes.

Oh, give over, Clem told himself crossly, turning from the window, sprawling back down on his bed. Anyone would think you were in love with her. And he knew he wasn't, despite the dizzy feeling when he'd held that long thick plait in his hand. It hadn't been that sort of dizziness, he thought sleepily, not love or sex or anything like that. Not a bit like when he'd had that crush on Paula Reeves back in Year Ten. It was—he didn't know what, he was too tired now to work it out. Strange, that's all, strange like Amy was. Mysterious and strange.

Chapter Thirteen

To call back a spirit, you first had to believe there were such beings to call. And however much she wanted to believe that people could come back, whatever she told Jess, Vida could never be quite sure.

Where did you go when you died? Did you go anywhere? Were you still really you? Perhaps you were nothing, perhaps you were gone for good. Vida couldn't bear that thought, and every morning when she woke doubt came tumbling over her in a long cold wave.

This morning the doubt was so bad she felt like crying, like pulling the doona over her head and going to sleep again. But she wouldn't, decided Vida fiercely; that would be giving in. And grabbing a book of ghost stories, wrapping the doona round her shoulders, she left the room and went trailing down the stairs.

Vida had a special place for reading: the old sofa in the

far corner of the back verandah, where no one ever came.

Only this morning someone did come. She'd hardly settled to her book when the screen door squeaked and Dad was standing there, his face a deep embarrassed pink above the collar of his shirt.

'You're up early,' he said to Vida.

'Yeah.'

'Reading?'

'Mmm.' Vida slipped her book beneath the doona before he saw the title and suggested she find something more cheerful to read. Mrs Mack did that all the time: 'silly rubbish' she called Vida's books.

'Aren't you cold out here?' Dad's warm fingers touched her cheek and Vida flinched; she felt lonely all the time, yet when anyone touched her or tried to talk she couldn't help shrinking away. 'I've got my doona.'

'Oh.' Dad drew his hand back but kept standing beside her sofa, hands in his pockets, rocking a little on his heels. 'Your dad's a shy man,' she remembered Mum saying once, and it had seemed funny back then, how a grown-up person could be shy. She'd thought Mum was kidding her.

He *was* shy though, she could see it now. He was a person who never knew what to say to them, and it was worse since Mum had got sick and he'd had to do the talking on his own.

'Um, Vida?'

She waited.

'About Katie . . .' he began.

Katie. Vida's lips narrowed in a thin straight line. If he was going to start nagging her about answering Katie's letters . . .

'I've been thinking, Vee. Why don't you ask Katie up for a few days, before school starts again?'

'She's on holidays.' She wasn't. Vida could tell from the address on the back of those last two letters that Katie was back from her Gran's.

'Oh well, when she gets back, eh?'

'Yeah, I'll ask her then.' She wouldn't though, no way; she didn't want Katie coming here, feeling sorry for her, trying to be kind.

'Right. Well . . .' Dad went on hovering.

'You'll be late for work,' Vida reminded him. It was a two-hour trip to his office in the city; he had to leave by seven.

'Work. You're right, I guess.' From the sound of his voice you'd think work didn't matter any more. 'Better be off, then.'

As he stooped to kiss her, Vida checked the buttons on his shirt. Buttons fastened in the wrong holes brought bad luck; anything could happen to him.

'What is it?'

'Oh, nothing.' He had them done up right; he'd be safe then. 'Bye, Dad. Seeya.'

'Seeya.' Halfway down the verandah he stopped and

turned round again. 'Vee, if there's ever anything, if you need me when I'm in the city, just ring, okay? Ring. I'm always there.'

'Sure,' she promised and he went at last, and Vida settled back down to her book. The ghost stories she was reading were true ones—it said so on the back—but not one of them convinced her. The people who told those stories could have been dreaming, she thought—or making things up like Evie Swann had done: pretending, showing off. She read on, turning the pages quickly, a tight feeling gathering in her chest because she wanted so badly to believe, to find just one story that sounded like it might be true.

And on page 124, Vida did find one. The lady who told it, a Mrs Stella Herbert, sounded really sensible, and she'd never believed in ghosts before. And who'd make up a ghost like Johnnie Minney, anyway? He was just a little boy in striped pyjamas who stood by Mrs Herbert's bed and asked her to call his mum. Mrs Herbert had tried but she couldn't seem to get the words out until the little boy took her by the hand and led her to the room next door.

The words had come easily there. 'Mama!' Mrs Herbert had called, feeling a little silly, 'Mama!'—and then Johnnie Minney had smiled blissfully at someone invisible standing in the doorway and Mrs Herbert hadn't felt foolish any more.

She'd been a visitor to that old English farmhouse where the ghost appeared. She hadn't known that long ago little

67

Johnnie Minney had died in the room next to hers, or that his illness had taken his voice away so he couldn't call his mum.

You wouldn't make up a story like that, would you? thought Vida. You simply wouldn't imagine it, so it had to be true.

She jumped up from the sofa and began to pace along the verandah with quick little happy steps. People *could* come back then; it wasn't nonsense, old wives' tales. They could come back, they could see you and talk to you. And you could talk to them— you could say you were sorry and they'd hear. Vida hugged the book tightly to her chest, she was smiling, she couldn't help it, her mouth curved upwards of its own accord and even her voice sounded smiley when she said out loud, 'It's true, it's true, it's true.'

Chapter Fourteen

But Mrs Mack didn't think so. 'Dreaming, that Stella Herbert was,' she pronounced, clashing the dishes loudly in the sink. 'Anyone can see: you can tell from the way she couldn't call that little boy's mum for him at first, how she kept trying and the words wouldn't come—'

'That's because she was in the wrong room,' argued Vida. 'She had to be in his old room, the one next door.'

'No.' Mrs Mack's orange curls bounced as she firmly shook her head. 'Listen, love, haven't you ever had those dreams where you're trying to do something ordinary, like getting dressed or packing a bag to catch a train— and you can't? Where you can't find your clothes, or your feet won't move and your fingers feel all thumbs? Or you try to talk and the words won't come? That's what happened there— it was only a dream she had.'

'I had a dream like that,' began Jess eagerly, and Vida

shouted, 'Who asked you? Mind your own business, you don't know anything!'

'Don't talk to your little sister like that, love,' Mrs Mack said mildly. 'And you should give over reading those ghost stories, Vida. All you're doing is scaring yourself and they're nonsense, anyway. Why don't you—' Mrs Mack didn't get to finish because Vida jumped up so violently her chair clattered backwards to the floor.

'Why do you have to spoil things?' she yelled at Mrs Mack.

'Eh?' Mrs Mack stepped back against the sink, her blue eyes round with surprise. 'What things? I didn't spoil anything, dear.'

'Yes you did! You always do! You don't believe people can come back, do you? Once they're dead. "Dead and gone", that's what *you'd* say. "Dead and gone!"'

Mrs Mack opened her mouth to reply, but again Vida didn't give her a chance. 'And I bet you don't believe in Heaven, either,' she rushed on. 'In angels and harps and the lion laying down with the lamb? You don't think that's where people go, nobody believes that any more.' Vida waved her arms wildly at the ceiling. 'How could there be a big green garden up there in the sky? And how could everyone fit in, even if there was? And what would they do all day and forever?'

Mrs Mack stood there, backed up against the sink, so upset she couldn't say a word. Jess felt a rush of sympathy.

She loved Mrs Mack; her solid blocky shape, the jaunty curls, the cheerful way she moved about the house. If she told Mrs Mack how she thought there might be a ghost girl following her, a girl dressed in blue who was slowly forming in the air, pushing her way into their world, Mrs Mack would laugh. 'You're imagining things, lovie,' she'd say. And then find Jess something interesting to do. When Jess was with Mrs Mack she felt safe.

But Mrs Mack didn't know how to make Vida feel safe. She seemed almost afraid of her.

'Well?' demanded Vida. 'What do you think happens when a person dies?'

'I—I believe there's something, dear.'

'Something!' Vida's voice rose again. 'I know what you believe! You think they just rot in the ground; that there's nothing left, just rotting, and maggots eating them, and worms crawling out of their eyes!' Vida was crying now, great rainy tears were streaming down her cheeks.

'Oh Vida,' Mrs Mack's broad face crumpled with a kind of pity. 'Of course I don't think that. I didn't mean to upset you, love—'

'I'm not upset!'

Mrs Mack held out her arms. Vida backed away.

'Get off! Leave me alone!' Vida could see tears in Mrs Mack's eyes but she wasn't going to say sorry to her, she wasn't. Mrs Mack was lucky, lucky—that's what Vida thought. She could go home in the evenings to her own house where everything was ordinary and there was no one lying sick and silent in a room upstairs. Mrs Mack didn't have to feel guilty and scared because she'd once done something terrible that nothing on earth could put right.

Cruel words burst from Vida's lips. 'I'm glad you're crying! And it's good you're standing near the sink because your silly tears can go down the plughole and it won't make a mess!'

And snatching her book from the table Vida dashed from the room, so fast she seemed all blurry round the edges, like a ghost . . .

Chapter Fifteen

Clem had woken up late that morning. His small room was hot and stuffy, bright sun streaming through the window, and yet he felt cold and shivery, with an odd little tingling right at the top of his head. He pulled the thin grey blanket closer round him; it was all he had on his bed. He wasn't sure where his doona was because he hadn't unpacked yet. He kept meaning to and then each day he forgot. Boxes lined the walls of his room, all his stuff from *Avalon* still inside them; he hadn't even hung up his clothes.

And they'd been here, what? Two months? Six weeks? He was getting really slack these days and his memory seemed full of unexpected little holes that made him feel uneasy. Why did he keep forgetting things? Try as he might, he couldn't remember the day they'd left *Avalon* or the trip up in the car. Had it been rainy or fine that morning? Had they driven straight up or stopped halfway? What had he thought when they'd turned in from the road and he'd seen the new house for the very first time?

He simply didn't know. He couldn't remember Christmas, either. Perhaps they hadn't had Christmas this year because of Mum being sick, and it had passed by like any other day. Was that it? When he looked back and tried to remember, his mind fuzzed over like an old photograph with all the details blurred away.

Down in the kitchen he heard Vida shouting. 'Get off! Leave me alone!' she was yelling. And something else he couldn't quite make out, about tears in the kitchen sink. Now she was rushing up the stairs; he always knew her footsteps because of those clattery boots she wore. She was crying.

'Vee!' He jumped from the bed and was out in the hall as she reached the top of the stairs. She brushed past him, running down the passage, slamming the door of the room she shared with Jess.

Now what? Clem stood outside the door, uncertain what to do. He couldn't leave her crying but he knew she wouldn't like him barging in; she'd been cross with him for weeks. He knocked, and when she didn't answer, he opened the door a little way and peered into the room.

She was sitting in the chair beside the desk, her back to him.

'Vee? What's the matter?'

She didn't turn her head, though she must have known he was standing there.

For the first time he noticed how thin she'd become: her bony shoulderblades poked through the flimsy cotton of her shirt like little wings. She didn't eat enough, her super-stitions got in the way of food. Yesterday at lunch she'd made the biggest fuss about Mrs Mack's sardines on toast. When you ate fish, Vida had lectured them, *any* kind of fish, you had to start at the tail and finish at the head, other-wise it brought bad luck. Mrs Mack had mashed the sardines up so you couldn't tell which end was which. Vida had pushed her plate away.

Poor Vee, he thought, walking softly across to her chair.

'Are you there?' she whispered.

'Yeah.'

Still she didn't turn round and Clem realised she was talking to that ouija board thing she'd brought home yesterday. He hated the way she was hunched over it, dead serious, expecting vital answers from a stupid piece of wood. He'd have liked to tell her it was only a party toy for idiots who wanted to spook themselves, but that would only make her mad. It was the reason she was cranky with him, like she was with Mrs Mack, because he thought that occult stuff of hers was rubbish and a waste of time.

He watched as she lifted the board and studied the sheet

of paper underneath, frowning because there were only squiggles there. She looked so disappointed, so grieved and desperate that Clem longed to comfort her, only he couldn't think of a thing to say she hadn't heard a hundred times from Dad and Dr Snow and Mrs Mack: how Mum would get better in time, though no one knew how much time, and that life might be a little better for her and Jess once school began again.

Once they got out of this house, Clem thought suddenly. Because there was something wrong with this house and it wasn't simply the hushing misery of Mum's illness, or the way they all missed their old life back home. There was something else he couldn't explain even to himself: a sense of being stuck, pinned down, so they couldn't get on with their lives . . .

And they needed to.

'I know everything seems awful right now, Vee,' he said gently, 'but it will change, you'll see.'

He was so close to her that the breath from his words must be tickling the back of her neck and still she wouldn't answer or turn round, only reached up and dabbed crossly at the skin beneath her hair, as if she was brushing an insect away.

It was too much. It always ended like this: getting mad with her. 'Oh, be like that if you want to,' he burst out. 'Talk to your old piece of wood then.'

And he stalked from the room, leaving her there, even

though he didn't want to, and wished he could help her somehow.

The image of those sharp shoulderblades sticking through her shirt went with him down the stairs, making him feel guilty and ashamed.

Chapter Sixteen

'You feel sorry for her, you try to help,' Clem told Amy outside in the garden, 'but she's so bloody-minded you end up getting furious—'

They could see Vida from their special place at the top of the lawn, but Vida couldn't see them. She was out on the terrace, sitting on the wooden garden seat, head bent over the book on her knee. She looked so very small and lonely down there that all Clem's anger drained away. Vida needed a friend.

He turned to Amy. 'Would you like to meet her?' he asked. 'And Jessie too, if she's around?'

Amy shook her head. 'I can't.'

'Why not?' He couldn't understand why Amy was so shy about coming down into the house and meeting his family. It was as if she didn't want anyone to see her, except for him.

'Is it your school?' he asked abruptly.

'School?' She looked really surprised at the question.

'Um, you are at school round here, aren't you? Some kind of boarding school? Is it against the rules or something, to come here? We wouldn't tell on you. I mean—' Clem stopped because suddenly his voice sounded strange. He could hear it in a way you never heard yourself talking, except perhaps on a tape, played back. There was an echoey noise in his ears too, like static on a telephone.

From a long way off he heard Amy asking, 'Are you all right?'

'My ears have gone funny.' He rubbed at them. 'There's a kind of buzzing, and everything sounds really far away.'

'That's because you don't belong here,' said Amy.

Clem stared at her. It seemed such an odd thing to say. It was true he couldn't get used to this new place and still thought of *Avalon* as his proper home, but that couldn't be what she'd meant. What could homesickness have to do with a buzzing in your ears? It had grown louder now, like a swarm of bees trapped inside his head.

'You don't belong here,' he thought she said again, and now there seemed to be something wrong with his eyes, because Amy's face loomed at him, so huge he couldn't see past it. There was only her face, and the sun, and the glittery trembling air.

The teasing familiarity of her features struck him again. Where had he seen her before? Or someone like her?

All at once it seemed important to know.

'You should come with me,' she said, and for the first time he felt afraid of her. What was she talking about?

'Come where?'

'Don't you know?'

Of course he didn't. Had she said something he'd missed, because of the noise in his ears?

'There's nothing to be afraid of, honestly.'

'Afraid?' he echoed.

She gazed at him earnestly. Her eyes looked so deep you might drown in them, be swept away. He wrenched his gaze from hers and looked upwards, towards the sky. A long line of grey cloud was snaking in from the west. Unsettled, the weather forecast had said this morning.

'Clem—'

He felt her hand on his arm.

'Clem, it's not good you're here. It's not good for you and it's not good for your mum.'

What? Had she really said that? He couldn't be sure because the dizziness he'd felt yesterday came sweeping over him again. It was worse this time, so intense it made him feel sick. He brushed her hand away and hunched over, his head down on his knees, waiting for it to pass.

And when it did, and he raised his eyes, Amy was gone. She simply wasn't there any more.

He could see the whole of the garden from there: the lawns and flowerbeds and paths, the long empty curve of the drive—and there wasn't a sign of her. How could she have gone out of sight so fast? The dizziness had only lasted for a minute; the line of grey cloud was still in exactly the same place above the trees, and down on the terrace Vida still sat in the same position, the book open on her knee. But now the buzzing in his ears had stopped, Clem noticed that everything else had gone quiet, the cicadas had stopped singing and the magpies too, a stillness had come over the garden. It was like being in a big glass jar with the stopper jammed in tight.

Was it him? Were his ears still playing up? He waggled his head and at once the silence broke: down at the house the screen door slammed and Mrs Mack came out onto the terrace. 'Lunch!' she called. 'Lunch is ready!' From somewhere inside he heard Jess's clear voice answer 'Coming!' and then Vida got up from the bench and her boots made a tapping sound as she walked slowly across the terrace towards the front door.

Lunchtime. That might be why Amy had run off so suddenly—at lunchtime she'd be missed back at her school.

Might be missed . . .

Clem tossed the damp sweaty hair back from his forehead. He didn't want to think about Amy, the way she'd vanished, left him, those weird things he thought she'd said. Not now, anyway.

Lunchtime already. He couldn't remember what he'd had for breakfast. Cornflakes? Eggs? Some more of Mrs

Mack's sardines on toast? Perhaps he'd forgotten to have any and that was why he'd started feeling bad. Or he might 'be coming down with something', like his Nan always used to say.

Cautiously, Clem got to his feet and began to walk down the slope towards the house, feeling oddly floaty and light, like you do when you've been ill for weeks and finally make it out of bed.

He didn't much fancy the idea of lunch. He'd skip it, Clem decided. He'd go and lie down in his room. He was tired and he didn't feel hungry at all.

Chapter Seventeen

It rained again that afternoon. In the reserve the dark trees swayed and bowed, water trickled down into the grassy hollow, but Amy went on sitting there, staring at the windows of the house. 'Clem,' she whispered. 'Clem, come out. Come with me.'

Clem didn't hear her, he'd fallen asleep in the room at the end of the hall, the rough grey blanket pulled around him.

Jess sat reading in her mother's room, her back to the window, trying not to think of ghosts.

Vida had taken the planchette from the wardrobe again and huddled over it; sheets of screwed up paper drifted to the floor. 'Stupid thing,' she said at last, 'why won't you work for me?'

A vision of Mrs Mack's crumpled face drifted into her mind. Mrs Mack couldn't have known how important it was for Vida to believe the story of Johnnie Minney was true; that ghosts came back, and you could speak to them. Vida knew she'd been unkind to her; she hadn't meant to be. She hated the way those angry furious feelings rushed over her, boiling up from deep inside. It frightened her.

If only she could talk to Mum. Mum would have been able to tell her if what she'd done that night at *Avalon* meant she really was to blame for everything. Mum would have known.

Mum had always been Vida's favourite person. People said you weren't supposed to have favourites in a family, but of course you did. She and Mum had been so alike: both tall and with the same dark hair and eyes, both quick impatient people, always in a hurry, always talking. Some weekend nights she and Mum had stayed up so late talking it would be getting light before they finally went to bed and they hadn't felt tired, either of them, not one little bit.

Vida couldn't talk to Dad in the same way; Mum was the person she'd shared her secrets with, the person who understood.

Only Mum was gone now. The woman who lay in the room down the hall wasn't the same person. She was a—a changeling, Vida thought wildly, one of those grey scabby silent things she'd read about, who crept round the world looking for a home, waiting to catch you when you weren't prepared and didn't know. Like when you sneezed—because when you sneezed your soul leapt out on your breath and if no one knew to say 'bless you' then it could fly away, and then the changeling could come creeping in.

Vida sighed. She knew Mum wasn't a changeling; she knew that was only stories. Mum was just a lady who'd had a breakdown and couldn't get well again. Or *wouldn't* get well.

Wouldn't.

Wouldn't try. And before Vida could stop it the angry rushy feeling started up in her chest again: she hated the way Mum lay there ignoring them, never helping, never caring—

Behind her the door opened quietly. She looked round and saw her sister standing there.

'What do *you* want?'

'I—I just wanted to tell you something,' stammered Jess.

Vida's eyes swerved at once to the planchette.

'No, not that,' said Jess quickly. 'I haven't changed my mind about that thing. I'm still not touching it, Vee.'

Vida leaned back in her chair. 'Okay,' she said coldly. 'So what do you want to *tell* me, little scaredy cat?'

Jess hesitated. She'd come because she couldn't bear Vida thinking those awful things she'd shouted in the kitchen; that stuff about maggots and rotting and worms crawling out of eyes. It was horrible. 'I think people might come back, Vee. Or at least,' she added hastily, 'I don't think they just die.'

'How do you know?'

Jess was silent. She wished she hadn't come, now. She

couldn't tell Vida about the ghost girl. She wasn't even sure she hadn't imagined her.

'How do you know?' repeated Vida.

'I just do,' said Jess helplessly.

'Then why won't you help me with this?' Vida touched the planchette lightly and at once the little wheels spun round: shee-sha, shee-sha—

Jess flinched at the sound. 'Because I don't think you should try to *bring* people back,' she said. 'It might be wrong. You might—you might get the wrong person.'

Vida glared at her. 'As if I would.' She stroked the gleaming yellow board. 'You can't tell me what to do.'

'Please, Vee,' whispered Jess, but Vida turned her head away.

Mrs Mack's voice came ringing up the stairs. 'Jessie! Want to come and help me roll the pastry for the apple pie?'

Apple pie was their dad's very favourite dessert.

'And—and Vida?' Mrs Mack's kind voice sounded more uncertain now. 'Vida, love?'

Vida blushed. She hadn't apologised for those cruel things she'd said.

'I'm staying here,' she told Jess. 'But you go. Everyone likes you.' Vida felt so miserable she couldn't stop adding spitefully, *'Be* her little pet.'

Tears shone in Jess's eyes. With a little gasp, she turned from the room and ran away down the stairs.

Chapter Eighteen

A blue hem.

And then a blue skirt.

'Soon you'll see more of me,' the ghost girl had whispered to Jess in her dream. 'You'll see a little bit, and then another little bit, until you see all of me, until you see my face.'

The blue skirt would become a dress.

'Dad,' she asked, 'why do ghosts wear clothes?'

'What?'

Jess and her father were walking in the garden, along a gravel path still damp and spongy from the rain. Bright drops hung on the bushes and the air smelled warm and spicy like the sweet steam from Mrs Mack's apple pies.

'You know, when you read about ghosts, they're always wearing clothes, gowns and cloaks and stuff. Skirts—'

'There aren't any ghosts, Jessie, that's all fairy tales.'

'I know,' Jess said quickly, because she didn't want to worry him, 'I know that, Dad. I was talking about stories, how ghosts in stories always wear clothes. And how could they? How could clothes come back when they're only things and haven't got any souls? They couldn't, could they?'

'Of course not.'

Jess nodded. Of course not. She'd worked that out herself, yet working it out didn't seem to help. Even after the peaceful hours she'd spent with Mrs Mack this afternoon, even with Dad beside her now, she couldn't stop herself from glancing back over her shoulder, fearfully . . .

Dad put his arm around her. 'And people can't come back either, Jessie,' he said sadly. 'Though sometimes we might wish they could.'

I don't, thought Jess. It was Vida who wanted that. It was Vida's wishing that had brought the ghost girl here.

'Wishing's how ghosts come back.' She spoke the thought aloud.

'Wishing?'

'They wish a sort of picture of themselves, Dad, that's why ghosts have clothes. It's pictures of clothes, in their mind, see? It's a ghost remembering how it used to look.' Jess could hear her voice getting faster, rushing like Vida's did. 'The ghost wishes really hard, and if there's a person here who's wishing too, then the ghost can get through, little bit by little bit. And then, they might hurt you. They might.'

'Jess, just wait a moment.' Dad crouched down beside her so his face was level with hers. 'Jessie, listen to me, sweetheart.'

Jess could hear him talking but she couldn't concentrate on what he said because she was thinking hard about how it might feel to be a ghost.

You'd be so very lonely; you'd be running up and down trying to get someone to see you, to hear. When Jess walked down a street people smiled at her and sometimes they said 'Hello'. If she spoke to them, asked a question or something, they answered her.

It wouldn't be like that if you were a ghost. Hardly anyone would see you and if they did they'd be scared like Evie Swann had been when she heard the ghost girl's voice.

Hopeless, that's how you'd feel, Jess thought with a small shiver. And you'd get to hate people for treating you so carelessly. You'd want to hurt them back.

Even a person you knew, someone who'd been gentle and funny and kind, who'd loved you, might be cruel and cold if they became a ghost. They might. She trembled.

'Jessie, listen, listen to me.' Dad was still crouching on the sodden path, his arms around her, trying to make her listen. 'Look, we haven't had an outing for ages, have we? And we should have, just a little one, don't you think?'

Jess nodded.

'So why don't we have a picnic this weekend, eh? There are lots of nice places round here, or we could even go down to the coast; it's not that far.'

'I don't want to go down the coast. I don't like the sea any more.'

'Oh. Okay then. Well, what about the Jenolan Caves? We haven't been there yet.'

'What about Mum?'

'Mrs Mack could come for the day. She'd look after Mum.'

Jess shook her head. They couldn't go without Mum. They couldn't leave her behind when she'd always come with them, when she was the one who'd made their picnics; cold chicken and special salads, fresh crusty rolls she'd got up really early to buy from the bakery.

Jess looked into her father's eyes and saw that he was thinking the very same thing: however much they wanted to go out, like ordinary families did, they couldn't go without Mum. They'd be pretending. Even if Mum didn't know about their picnic, didn't care, they'd still feel mean inside.

'All right then.' Dad got to his feet, still holding her hand. 'You're a nice little girl, Jessie, you know that? I'm proud of you. And when Mum's well enough to come with us, we'll go.'

They stood close together, looking up at the sky. It was getting dark now. The clouds left over from the rain were edged with gold, big violet spaces in between where the stars were starting to shine. Clem once told her the spaces between those stars were so big it would take a lifetime to cross between, perhaps a hundred lifetimes. And beyond those stars were wider spaces, on and on and on; more stars so far away you couldn't see them, more stars, more spaces.

It made your head go whizzy, even thinking of it.

Chapter Nineteen

'Our uniform's this really awful green,' Jess told her mum. 'That green like wheelie-bins, you know? And it's got buttons, too, all down the front, like those frocks old ladies wear. Would you like to see it, Mum? Will I show it to you?'

Of course she doesn't want to see it, thought Vida wearily. Mum didn't want to see anything that had to do with them.

'There's a hat, too,' Jess went on. 'You had a hat, didn't you, Mum, when you went to school?'

Vida slumped down in her chair. Say something, she willed the silent woman lying on the bed. The tight angry feeling began to gather in her chest.

'Mum?' whispered Jess. 'You had a hat. It's in that photo in the album, the one of you and your best friend. What was her name? Annie? Was it Annie, Mum? You know, the one who went to India with her family . . .' Jess stopped, remembering suddenly that Mum's friend had never come back from there.

'I knew she'd died,' Mum had said as they'd studied the photograph. 'I knew when she didn't write to me. But it took me months to go to her church and find out for sure. I suppose I wanted to keep on hoping . . .'

Jess changed the subject quickly. Dr Snow said Mum might hear them, and being reminded of her friend might make her sad. 'Look!' She held her hand out, spreading the fingers wide. 'Look Mum, I've stopped biting my finger-nails. You told me and told me, remember? When we were back at *Avalon*, and I kept on biting them, but now I've stopped, honest. See?'

Answer her, why don't you? raged Vida silently. You could tell Mum anything, she thought, and she wouldn't turn a hair. You could tell her about the nightmare tele-phone, or how you were too scared to open your best friend's letters—you could even tell her what you'd done that night at *Avalon*, and she wouldn't even care.

The angry rushy feeling swelled in Vida, rose up into her throat. How come Mum got to lie there while the rest of them had to manage, do all the ordinary things like moving house and starting at a new school and trying to find friends? Do it all no matter how they felt inside?

Having a breakdown was easy.

'See how there's these little white rims on top?' she heard

Jess begging. 'See, Mum? I'll be able to cut them soon.'

Silence.

Jess dropped her hand and her cheeks flushed with the kind of embarrassment people feel when they tell a total stranger a secret they should have kept to themselves.

It was too much for Vida: the hot rushy feeling spilled right over, all the anger and loneliness, bitter guilt and grief. She leapt from the chair and lunged towards the bed.

'Look, why don't you? You've got eyes. They still work, don't they? Even if nothing else does. You can see, at least.'

Her voice wasn't loud. Downstairs in the study her father didn't hear it, or Clem lying on his bed in the room at the end of the hall. Yet Vida's whisper held all the violence of a scream.

Jess tugged at her sister's arm. 'Vee, don't, don't!'

But Vida couldn't stop; all that stuff inside her was like something bad she'd swallowed and had to chuck right up. 'Mum, listen! It's me! It's *us*—Vida and Jess. Talk to us, we're still here. Remember us, Mum? Don't we matter any more? Don't you even care?'

'Leave her alone,' cried Jess. 'She can't help it, she's sick. I don't mind if she doesn't listen, really I don't. It's not important. Please, Vee.'

Vida's hand rushed up to her mouth, dark violet shadows bloomed beneath her eyes. She rushed from the room, down the hall into the bathroom, slamming the door behind her. Jess raced after her, Clem ran out from his

94

room. They stood outside the bathroom listening to the awful sounds of Vida being sick.

'Vee?'

'Are you all right?'

'Want me to get Dad?'

'Vee?'

The retching stopped, the toilet flushed, a tap squeaked and water ran into the basin. 'I'm all right,' came Vida's choky voice. 'Just leave me alone, will you? Can't a person even be sick in peace?'

* * *

Sarah heard her daughters' voices dimly, Vida's angry, Jessie sounding scared. 'Don't you even care?' Vida was crying, 'Don't you even care?'

Not yet, Sarah thought, not yet, please, drifting back into her safe and happy place.

They were talking about getting married, she and her best friend. In the sunny upper quad, getting married had always seemed a long way off, but Josie Peters in fourth year had just got engaged and Josie was only two years older than them.

'Just think,' said Sarah. 'Somewhere there's these two boys we'll marry, we'll spend all our lives with them, and they don't even know about us. They don't know what we look like or where we live or who our friends are, or anything.'

The other girl nodded. 'And we don't know about them. Not anything. It's weird, isn't it?'

'Really weird.'

'Let's keep on being friends when we get married, okay?'

''Course we will.'

'People don't, sometimes. My mum, she doesn't know any of the girls she went to school with any more, even her very best friend, Lizzie. She doesn't know where Lizzie lives now or anything. She says once you get married you lose touch and once you have kids you never have time to think of anything else.'

'We wouldn't be like that.'

'No.'

'Promise?'

'Promise.'

They locked little fingers, and then Sarah thought of something better. She took the small gold safety pin from her belt and they pricked each other's thumbs, pressing the small bright beads of blood together.

'Friends always.'

'Forever.'

They'd watch out for each other, they promised. All their lives.

Chapter Twenty

Vida lay awake in the dark, afraid to go to sleep in case she heard the nightmare telephone.

Of course she'd hear it, after saying those awful things to Mum. She'd hated her tonight. Yes, just for a moment, she'd really hated Mum. Now the hate had melted away and she simply felt afraid. What if Mum had heard? She might have; you simply didn't know.

She'd make it up to her, Vida promised silently. She'd . . . she'd make a spell for Mum; there was a charm in one of her books to protect sick people and keep them safe. All you needed was a candle and she could get one from the craft shop in Springdale tomorrow, they had lots of candles there. She'd catch the first bus, the very first.

Vida yawned. She was very tired and her stomach felt sore and achey from being sick, but every time her eyelids drooped she forced them open because she was so scared of that telephone. She might even hear Mum's voice tonight—that soft 'hello'—and see the white curtains billowing out at the window of her old room.

That was the very last moment, thought Vida sleepily, when those curtains blew out—the very last moment of their old life before everything went wrong.

But Vida didn't hear the telephone that night. She fell asleep gently and dreamed she was with Katie, back home. It was a Friday afternoon in winter, they were walking home from hockey practice, planning what they were going to do on Saturday afternoon. 'We could go to the mall,' suggested Katie, but Vida said she was sick of the mall.

'What about a film in town? Will your mum drive us to the ferry?'

'Yeah, only then Jess'll want to come—' Vida broke off because she could see Clem ahead of them, getting off the Manly bus with his friend Liam and the other boys from his school. He rolled his eyes when he spotted her and Katie, raised one arm, swept his schoolcap from his head and bowed to them in the middle of the street. Bowed grandly, without a thought for the stares of passers-by.

'Hello, ladies,' he greeted them. Katie giggled and then they all walked home together, across the traffic lights, down Lanscombe Road and round the corner into Curzon Street where Katie turned off to her house.

Vida smiled in her sleep. It was so lovely, being back there.

Chapter Twenty-one

When she was quite certain Vida was asleep, Jess crept out of bed and tiptoed down the hall. She wanted to see Mum.

The hall was long and shadowy; a cold little wind blew up the stairs. From the study below she could hear the soft tap of Dad's computer but up here everything was still and quiet. Jess shivered. She hated this house, it was the kind of house where anything might happen. She wouldn't have been surprised to look behind her and find the walls had shifted, the stairway melted away into the air.

Mum was asleep. Jess could tell from the way she was lying; half on her side, one arm flung up across the pillow, her fingers gently curled. Vida slept like that.

Jess leaned over the bed. 'Vee didn't mean it, Mum,' she whispered. 'She didn't mean those things she said. She gets—' Jess paused, because how did Vida get? Angry? That was how it sounded when she started going on at you, when she jumped up and began yelling like she'd done this morning in the kitchen with Mrs Mack.

But tonight in Mum's room, Jess had seen something else. Vida had been angry, but she'd also been scared. Jess had seen it in her eyes, the flicker of fright beneath that hard hot glare. Jess had never imagined Vida being scared, how could she? Vida was her big sister, and back home Vida had always looked after her.

Jess could still remember her very first day at school: how she'd sat in the big classroom with all the other kids, ready to start crying because she'd never been away from Mum before. And then she'd looked up and seen Vida's face at the window, just the top part of her face because the window was very high, Vida's black untidy fringe and big dark eyes. But that had been enough: Jess had known her big sister was there, checking up to see she was all right. And she *had* been all right after that; she hadn't started crying anyway, and lots of the other kids had.

Vida had always been the brave one; now it was starting to get different.

'Vida's scared, Mum,' Jess whispered. 'That's why she said those things to you, she can't help it, but then afterwards, she's sorry. She's really sorry.' And though it sounded strange to hear herself say this, Jess added, 'I'll look after her. I will, Mum. You don't have to worry. I'll watch out for her.'

100

She stepped back from the bed and her foot touched something soft and clingy; it was only Mum's shawl, the blue one with the little mirrors Dad had bought for her when she came home from hospital. Jess picked it up and spread it gently over the doona so Mum was all covered up in rich deep blue, like a person wrapped in a night time sky with little stars shining in it.

Out in the hall she paused to look through the window. Down on the terrace the big floodlight glittered on pools of water left by the rain. Two smaller puddles by the garden seat had the shape of a pair of shoes.

They *were* shoes. Vida must have left her boots outside, Jess thought when she saw them, but then she remembered Vida taking her boots off back in their room and the two little thumps they'd made as she tossed them onto the floor.

Those shoes out there weren't Vida's. Jess had never seen them before: a pair of shiny black lace-ups with small square polished heels.

And as she watched, one of them moved. It glided forward in a little step and then the other slid up to meet it, so they were standing neatly side by side. Above them Jess could make out a pair of slender legs in black tights and the hem of a skirt which looked grey in the night, but would really be bright blue.

It was true, then. The tiny hairs rose on the back of her neck, she felt the very breath in her turn cold. She hadn't been imagining things; she was really seeing a ghost out there. Little bit by little bit, as the voice had said in her dream.

And now as she watched, the rest of the dress appeared, slipping softly from behind the air: a full skirt with a square-necked bodice, a white blouse beneath it—the girl was wearing a tunic, like Mum used to wear at school!

The floodlight on the terrace made the white blouse gleam, the long sleeves, the pointed collar . . . Jess screwed her eyes shut, she didn't want to see that face, the cruel goblin face, twisted up with spite and jealousy.

She had to look though; she had to know what was watching them out there.

There was no face. Above the girl's gleaming collar there was only air, and the slope of the lawn behind it, dark bushes, the friendly shapes of trees. The sight of that dark empty space was terrifying, yet in the centre of the terror Jess felt a small sharp stab of relief, because the girl wasn't whole, not yet. And that might mean she couldn't do what she'd come to do.

And what was that? What did she want from them? Thoughts tumbled through Jess's mind with frightening speed, while all the while her eyes stayed fastened on that girl outside.

Sometimes ghosts did terrible things, like the one in Vida's book who'd taken the child away. But others were harmless, like little Johnnie Minney who'd only wanted someone to call his mum.

Johnnie Minney's house had been old. Houses where ghosts appeared were always old; places where people had died or bad things had happened in the past. This house was nearly new. The family before them, the Robinsons, had built it themselves and moved away after only twelve months. Jess had met the Robinsons when she'd come with Dad to see the house. They'd had a little girl called Sally, who was three years old. Had the Robinsons seen that ghost out there and been afraid for Sally? Was that why they'd moved?

They hadn't seemed like haunted people, they hadn't seemed scared as they would have been if a ghost girl was after their child. They'd been happy and excited about the house they'd bought down in the city. 'It's even got a view of the harbour,' Mr Robinson had told them. 'If you climb on the roof, that is.'

No, it was one of this family the girl out there was after. Hadn't she followed Jess from Willow Street?

The ghost was standing very still in the middle of the lawn, and though she didn't have a face Jess could tell from the way her blue tunic was turned that the girl was staring at the windows of their house. Not this window outside Mum's room—so she hadn't come to take Mum away. She was gazing towards the other end of the house, where there was only the small spare room, and the bedroom beside it, where she and Vida slept.

Where Vida was sleeping now.

Vida. Vida was the one she wanted. That would be why, for all the wishing that had brought her, Vida had never seen her. A ghost would be sly and cunning if she wanted to snatch someone away.

'Leave us alone,' Jess whispered, and the moment she spoke the ghost began to vanish like she'd done in the street yesterday. Only now it took longer because there was more of her to go: not just a tiny slip of hem but those shiny shoes and black stockings, the old-fashioned tunic and stern white blouse. She was almost gone now, only one slender arm was left and a small hand held up as though she was waving, pretending to be a friend. What would happen if that hand caught yours and held it tight? Would you vanish too, sucked into the slips and cracks inside the air?

Jess shuddered again and then all at once she felt a sudden icy calm. 'You're not getting my sister,' she whispered. 'Because I won't let you, ever; I'm going to watch out for her.'

Chapter Twenty-two

'Dad?' Jess edged round the door of the study: the big desk was crowded with books and bulging files, the computer hummed softly, but the chair was empty and her heart gave a small sick lurch. 'Dad?'

'I'm here.' His warm voice came from the small sofa in the corner where he sat with another file open on his knee. 'Had a bad dream?'

'No, it's not that.' Jess sat down beside him.

'What then? Not still thinking about ghosts, are you?'

She wanted so much to tell him what she'd seen. But he mightn't believe her. And he looked so tired, too. He had so much work and he worried about Mum all the time. He sat with Mum for hours, reading to her, trying to get her to talk, coaxing her to eat a little more.

Jess couldn't tell him how she saw a ghost girl because

then he'd worry about her too. He'd think there was something wrong with her.

'Eh? Still thinking about ghosts?'

'No,' she lied. 'I was wondering about those people who lived here before us.'

'The Robinsons? What about them?'

'They built this house, didn't they? So why did they move away so soon? Was it because of their little girl?'

'Well, it was in a way, yes—'

'Was something after her? Trying to take her away?'

'Of course not.' Dad ruffled her hair. 'You've been reading too many of Vida's stories, haven't you? It was that long train trip to the city, Jessie. It got too much for them. By the time Mr Robinson got home from work their little girl was already in bed asleep. He never saw her except at weekends, and he didn't think that was right.'

'Was that all?'

Dad smiled at her. 'That's enough, isn't it? I wouldn't be very happy if I never got to see you. The Robinsons loved this place, they'd have stayed on if they could.'

'Oh.'

'What's the matter? Don't you like this house?'

Jess leaned into his shoulder. 'It's okay.'

'Would you like to have your own room, like you did back home? There's plenty of spares, you know. You could even have this room, I could move my things upstairs.'

'No, it's all right, Dad.' She had to stay with Vida now, she had watch out for her.

'It snows here in winter, you know. Just think, you've never seen snow before and in a few months time you'll have your own snowy garden.'

She couldn't imagine it. She had a sudden vision of the back garden at *Avalon*, the brown prickly summer grass, the red canna lilies blazing by the fence, and she couldn't stop the words bursting from her lips, 'I wish we could all go back to *Avalon*.'

Dad ruffled her hair again. 'You know it's rented out. We could have stayed, only I thought when—well, sometimes, when a bad thing happens, the place where you were happy can be sadder than a new one, because it keeps reminding you . . .'

'I know,' said Jess quickly, 'and I didn't mean go back *really*, Dad; I meant a sort of wish, you know? Like magic, us all being back there like it was before—before Mum got sick and everything. And sometimes it seems like you could—everything feels sort of thin, like you could walk right through and be back. There's a kind of funny shimmery feeling.' Jess lifted her head and saw the lines between his eyebrows deepen; she'd gone and worried him after all.

'But I know we can't, Dad. Go back. I know.'

'We will some day, Jessie, I promise. When Mum gets better.'

She squeezed his hand so tight she felt the bones, and that brought the drowning poem into her head: *Full fathom five thy father lies; Of his bones are coral made . . .*

Outside it had begun to rain again, heavily. It crashed onto the roof and rattled down the drainpipe, splashing onto the hard stones of the terrace below. The wind rushed at the window, moaned and prowled around the house.

Like a stormy night at *Avalon*, Jess thought, when the sea turned angry and wild. Imagine that cold sea flooding over you, sucking you down, lifting you up again. Then right down so you were gone, swept away and could never come home again.

Oh, what would it be like to drown? Jess glanced at her father's tired face. That was another question she couldn't ask him. Not ever.

Chapter Twenty-three

The moment Clem woke next morning he thought of Amy. The way she'd vanished, those strange things she'd said to him.

'Come with me.' Come where? Was she planning to run away from school and needed him for company? She didn't seem the type; Amy was what his Nan would have called 'a nice girl', and nice girls didn't run away from anywhere.

What had she meant when she'd said it was bad for him to stay here, and bad for his mum as well? He didn't know, but her words had frightened him. How could he be scared of some poor kid, no older than Vida, who'd been dumped at school for the holidays? Was she at school, though? *Was* she? Clem screwed his hands into fists and pressed the knuckles against his forehead, hard.

Why had he suddenly begun to suspect that Amy

mightn't be at school round here? Despite that uniform she wore? That she might have come from somewhere else, some place he didn't want to think about, the place she wanted him to go? And why did he feel, in some secret part of his mind, that the strange things she'd said mightn't be strange at all, but have some clear simple meaning he was afraid to recognise?

Clem shivered, he felt cold again, though the sun was pouring through the window, so high in the sky that he knew he'd woken up late again, like he seemed to keep on doing these days. And when he sat up, pushing his troubled thoughts aside, he found he'd slept in his clothes again, the same clothes he'd been wearing for ages: his grey jeans and the old blue sweatshirt he used for sailing, which after all this time still kept the faint briny smell of the sea.

His gaze slid towards the dusty boxes lined up against the walls; he still hadn't unpacked them. He'd never been this sloppy back at home; the sadness and trouble in this house seemed to drain his energy, making the simplest little tasks impossible to do. If he kept on like this, so dozy and muzzy in the mornings, fighting the urge to tumble back to sleep, how was he ever going to manage when the term began? He was still going to his old school at Manly—no one had told him different, anyway—so he'd have to get up really early to catch the train with Dad. He'd be in Year Twelve too. He had to get himself organised, make a start on that unpacking . . .

But when he got out of bed and looked around, such a cold aching loneliness flooded through him that he ran from the room and hurried down the stairs.

The washing machine was thumping in the laundry and he could hear Mrs Mack's voice above it, warbling some cheerful old song. In the kitchen the breakfast dishes had been washed and put away but that didn't matter, it wasn't food he needed, it was company. 'Jess!' he shouted, 'Vida!' hurrying from room to room, fetching up on the terrace where he called their names across the garden, over and over until he realised it was useless. They'd gone some-where, caught the early bus into Springdale probably, since there was nowhere else to go.

'You don't belong here,' Amy had said, and today the garden looked so empty and abandoned it did seem like that. Almost as if their family had never come to live here, thought Clem, were dreams or shadows in someone's mind, while their real selves were back at *Avalon* living their ordinary lives. His gaze swept over the lawn and up to the grassy hollow. He knew Amy would be waiting there, and the sense of that waiting filled him with such uneasiness that he turned and hurried back inside the house.

It was dead quiet in the hall. The washing machine had stopped; Mrs Mack must be out in the back yard hanging up the clothes. Clem paused beside the telephone table; Vida's letters from Katie still sat there unopened, stacked neatly in a pile. He picked one up and turned it over in his hand. Why on earth didn't Vida answer them? Open them, even? Katie had been her very best friend.

With a sudden little jolt Clem remembered that *he* had a best friend back there too.

Liam. He dropped Katie's letter back onto the table and sifted through the other envelopes lying there: junk mail, a couple of bills for Dad, a Christmas card from the estate agent that no one had bothered to open. Nothing from Liam. He knew Liam's family went away for Christmas, but they always came back in the first week of January because Liam's dad had to start work again. Liam would certainly be home by now.

Clem picked up the handset and pressed the familiar numbers: there was no ringing at the other end, only a kind of static, and behind it, a strange tense silence that sounded like an indrawn breath. Liam's phone was out, it must be. Clem hung up.

How come he'd never given a thought to Liam these past weeks? Vida mightn't have answered Katie's letters but she hadn't forgotten about her, Katie hadn't dropped from Vida's mind like Liam had dropped from his. Had he given Liam their new address and telephone number? He couldn't remember and now he thought about it he couldn't remember saying goodbye to him either.

When was the last time he'd seen Liam? He'd been with him at the school athletics carnival but that was ages back, in October, before Mum had got sick, before they'd ever guessed they'd be moving up to the hills. He must have seen Liam after that, lots of times . . .

A chill stole over him; he was getting frightened of these ratty little holes in his memory, as if moths had got inside his brain.

Concentrate, Clem told himself. Think back. When had he last seen Liam? He stared at the bowl of red geraniums Mrs Mack had placed beside the telephone. Their dazzling crimson reminded him of the canna lilies in the back yard of *Avalon*, the way they blazed up against the old grey wooden fence. He couldn't remember the last time he'd seen his best friend but every detail of their old back yard was vivid: the scrubby grass, worn away in patches from their cricket games, the clothesline, Dad's old shed, those canna lilies . . .

He could go there.

Of course he could. He needed company, and what better company could there be than Liam?

And yet—why hadn't he thought of it before, when he'd been homesick for so long? He'd fallen into the habit of thinking he could never go back to *Avalon*, and he couldn't understand how he'd got that idea. *Avalon* wasn't on the moon, it was down there on the other side of the city, a couple of hours away.

Clem checked the clock up on the wall—9.40. The Springdale bus would pass the gate at ten; he could be at Liam's place a little after one.

They could spend the afternoon together, hang out round the suburb like they used to do, walk down Clem's old street, past *Avalon*. Simply to see the old house again would be so good. Why had he felt he couldn't? It was this place, he thought wildly, scowling down the long shining length of the hall, this place did stuff to you; it made you feel feeble and afraid. He grabbed the pen to leave a note— he was going to *Avalon*. He was going and nothing could stop him. The pen didn't work and he didn't have time to look for another: it hardly mattered because he could ring Mrs Mack from Liam's place. With the long summer evenings he'd be home before dark anyway. Before they'd even noticed he was gone.

Chapter Twenty-four

There were so many candles in the craft shop that Vida found it hard to choose. White or coloured? Scented or plain? Which would be best? In her books they never told you things like that; the people who wrote them left out details because they expected you to know. There were times when Vida thought this might be why her spells and incantations never worked; at others she felt it was because what she'd done back at *Avalon* was so terrible no spirit would ever listen to her. She took a red candle from the shelf and then put it back again. White, she decided, she'd get a plain white candle because they mightn't have had coloured candles when those old spells were written down.

'What do you want a candle for?'

Vida looked round irritably. Jess was right behind her, treading on her heels.

'Vee? Why do you want a candle? It's not to call spirits up, is it? Because I think—'

'I don't care what you think! It's none of your business anyway! Will you just stop hovering and leave me alone?' Vida pointed to the door. 'Go and wait outside.'

Jess didn't move.

'Go on! Wait on that bench, see?' Vida waved through the window towards the courtyard outside the library.

Jess didn't want to leave her sister on her own, but Vida's voice was so loud and angry that the lady behind the counter was glaring at them both.

Reluctantly, Jess left the shop. And she found she could still watch out for Vida from the bench in the courtyard, because the door of the craft shop was propped open to catch the morning breeze. Her sister's slight figure was plainly visible, moving slowly along the shelves.

'Hello, love.'

Jess looked up, startled, and saw Evie Swann, all dressed up and carrying a big bunch of yellow roses wrapped in crinkly tissue paper. 'Off to see my new grandchild,' she announced. 'And guess what? My daughter's gone and called her Eva, after me.' Evie Swann smiled proudly; she looked so pleased that Jess couldn't help smiling back at her.

'Mind if I sit down with you for a bit and take the weight off my feet? My train's not due for a while, and I'm not very comfortable in these high heels. Still, you've got to dress up for town, haven't you?'

Jess made room along the seat and Evie Swann sat down beside her, smoothing her skirt and setting the yellow roses carefully on her lap. 'All on your own today?'

'My sister's in there.' Jess pointed across the street. 'She's buying a candle.'

'A candle, eh?' Evie Swann peered across at the shop. 'Well, she'll have plenty of choice in there, I'll bet.' She turned back to Jess. 'She's all right, is she?'

'All right?'

'Your sister. She left so suddenly the other day, we thought there might be something wrong.'

Jess felt her face grow hot, remembering how suddenly Vida had rushed them away. 'Oh no! It's, she—we had to go home,' she stammered. 'I'm sorry if we were rude.'

'Of course you weren't!' Evie Swann squeezed Jess's hand. 'I didn't mean anything like that, heaven's sake! But to tell you the truth, love, I'm glad I ran into you today. I've been worried about you and your sister.'

'Worried?'

'About that silly old seance of ours. I keep thinking we might have frightened you—frightened your sister anyway, because she seemed so upset.'

'It wasn't you,' said Jess quickly. 'I mean, it wasn't the seance.'

'It's been on my conscience, love. Perhaps I shouldn't have let two young girls come to something like that, only I didn't think for a moment it'd do any harm. Nothing's ever really happened before, and then, would you believe it? That very day I go and hear a voice, of all things! I'm not a real medium, you know. I'm not even psychic, or at least I've never thought so.' She smiled broadly. 'Not a seventh child of a seventh child—poor old Mum only had the three of us.'

'Did you hear a voice, honestly?' The question jumped out before Jess could stop it; she simply had to know. Because if Evie Swann wasn't really sure—if there was even the slightest chance she might only have imagined that voice, then, all along, Jess might have been imagining too. Even though she'd been so certain last night that the ghost girl was really there. Even though, at this very minute, she was afraid she might see her again through the doorway of the craft shop, standing next to Vida, holding out her hand.

You could imagine something and think that it was real, Jess knew that. On the day before they left *Avalon*, standing by herself on the pebbly strip of beach beside the jetty, Jess had thought she'd seen Dad's little boat, the *Sarah Jane*, out there on the bay. It hadn't looked made-up, not a bit like a boat you'd dreamed. It had been quite clear and solid, sitting on the water, its white sail billowing in the breeze, just like those times when Dad and Clem had gone sailing and she and Mum and Vida had seen them coming home across the bay. But it had been a dream of course, because it couldn't have been the *Sarah Jane*.

'Well, to be honest, love,' Evie Swann paused, searching Jess's face. 'You're not scared, are you, dear? Scared of the supernatural?'

Jess shook her head, hoping the lie didn't show.

'All right then.' Evie Swann looked down at the yellow roses on her lap, and gently stroked the edge of a petal with one finger. 'I've thought about it a lot,' she said slowly, 'gone over and over it in my mind, you know how you do when something's bothering you?'

'Oh, yes!'

'And I think I did, I'm sure it was real, that voice I heard. Oh, I've no doubt about it, because it was the *kind* of voice, see? The way it sounded so close, like there was this poor girl standing there next to me trying to tell me something. And the way everything—' Evie Swann raised a hand and smoothed it over the air— 'just slipped away, went still. I couldn't hear a thing else, not a breath, only her.'

'Oh.' Jess's last hope flickered away. She knew what Evie Swann said was true. She'd felt that peculiar stillness herself, each time she'd seen the ghost girl.

'But it's all right, love,' Evie Swann reassured her. 'That's what I wanted to tell you and your sister, in case you felt scared. There's nothing to worry about, because even if I did hear some kind of ghost—and it's a funny old world, isn't it? you never know—I'm absolutely sure she wasn't bad.'

'Bad?'

'She didn't mean any harm. Not a speck of it in her, that's what I felt. I don't have any idea what she wanted or why she spoke to me but she was a nice little thing, I'm quite sure of that.'

Jess wasn't. In a low voice she said, 'She might have been pretending.'

'Pretending?' Evie Swann sounded shocked at the idea. 'Oh no! She was so bothered, wasn't she, poor little thing? "I'm so hopeless", that's what she said. It sounded like she'd been given something to do, something really hard, and she couldn't figure out how to set about it and didn't have anyone to help. No, she meant no harm, I'd stake my life on it. So you're not to worry, see?' She patted Jess's cheek. 'Well, I'd better be off now, love, my train's nearly due.'

Evie Swann got to her feet, smoothing her skirt down, gathering up her roses and her bag. 'And look, dear,' she added, 'if you and your sister ever need anyone to talk to or something, I'm always there, you know—34 Willow Street, you remember the address?'

Jess nodded. 'Thank you,' she said awkwardly. 'And—and have a good time at your daughter's place.'

'Oh, I will, love. Wish I could take you with me, you and your big sister . . .'

Jess watched her cross the road towards the station, pink dress and yellow roses bright in the tired summer street. Evie Swann was so kind. And perhaps that was why

Jess couldn't believe what she'd said about the ghost girl meaning no harm. It would be so very easy for a cunning jealous ghost to trick someone as unsuspecting as Evie Swann.

Chapter Twenty-five

'Day return to—' Clem stopped short and began to drum his fingers on the polished wooden sill outside the ticket window. 'Day return to—' Would you believe it? He couldn't remember the name of his old suburb, the place he'd lived in all his life; it had slipped down into one of those mothy holes inside his head.

The man at the window stared at him blankly while Clem struggled to retrieve the name. It started with a B, he remembered that at least. Barrenjoey? No, that was the name of the peninsula and the road that ran down its spine. Bilgola Beach? Not Bilgola, that was further up the coast, but his suburb had the name of a beach in it too. A beach . . .

The place itself was achingly clear in his mind: the bay on one side, the beach on the other, the shopping centre and the pattern of the streets. *Avalon* itself, the big white

house with green windowsills and a green front gate—
he and Dad had painted them last summer—the blue
hydrangeas down the side, the canna lilies. Colours glowed
vividly inside his head, but he still couldn't find the name.

'It's on the peninsula,' Clem explained, 'this place I want
to go to—down past Narrabeen.'

The blank look stayed fixed on the ticket seller's face,
as if he'd never heard of Narrabeen. Perhaps he was one of
those locals Mrs Mack had told them about, who'd never
been into the city in his life.

'The Northern Beaches, you know? Towards Palm
Beach.' Clem took a breath. 'You get the bus from Manly.'
The guy must know Manly, everybody did, like they knew
Bondi. Manly, where he and Liam took the bus from school.
That bus! When Clem thought of the way it turned at the
top of Greycliffe Road and you looked down and saw the
lagoon shining and the waves crashing in on Queenscliff
Beach, a fierce ache of longing stabbed right through him.

He'd be on that bus in a couple of hours, if he could only
persuade this guy to sell him a ticket. 'Just give me a day
return to Manly then,' he said.

But as he spoke a woman with a little girl came bustling
to the counter, pushing him aside. 'One and a half return
to Penrith,' she said, and the ticket guy got moving right
away.

The little girl stared at Clem, tugging at her mother's
skirt. 'Mum,' she whispered, 'Mum, there's someone there.'

123

Her mum had their tickets now and grabbed her by the hand. 'Come on, Sophie, the train's nearly here.'

Clem could hear it too, and a panic rose in his chest as he stepped to the window again. 'Day return to Manly, please.' He heard his voice sounding queer and distant, and the ticket seller obviously couldn't hear him because he slid the window shut, picked up his flag and hurried out through the small side door. A breeze stirred the warm air of the waiting room and people Clem hadn't noticed began to move forward onto the platform: two men in business suits, a gang of school-kids, a plump lady in a pink dress with a big bunch of yellow roses who stared at Clem for a moment with that same puzzled look Mum sometimes gave him, as if she was surprised to see him there.

Mum. He'd forgotten to say goodbye to Mum.

The whistle sounded, the man held up his flag; slowly, the train began to move. There was still time for Clem to jump on and he could pay at the other end, only now the dizziness he'd felt yesterday in the garden with Amy came surging back, and the strange high buzzing in his ears.

His whole body felt weak; Clem slumped down with his back against the wall.

He wasn't going then.

In the back of his mind he'd known that all along. There was a reason he couldn't go back to *Avalon*, a reason he'd forgotten, which lay in one of those deep frightening holes in his mind. What was it?

As he sat there, something dark and heavy seemed to shift in his head and he almost had the answer—then the dark thing shifted back and it was gone.

Clem looked round dazedly. The platform was empty now, the ticket seller had gone back to his room. Clem staggered to his feet. He couldn't stay here.

Outside the station the Hillcrest bus was leaving. As it swept past, he saw Jess's face pressed against the window. She was looking back towards the street so she didn't see him, and Vida didn't either, her head was bent over a book. The next bus didn't leave for an hour and he didn't want to wait that long. He needed to get back to Mum.

It was three kilometres to his house. His head was spinning and he felt like he was going to be sick, but he could walk it. He had to; there was something he needed badly to tell Mum.

Chapter Twenty-six

A little way past the Whittakers' green cottage Clem had to stop and sit down on the grassy bank beside the road.

Summer flu, he thought. That must be what was wrong with him. Jess had caught summer flu last year and Mum had fed her glucose and water in tiny little sips because she couldn't keep anything down. Flu would be why he felt so weak and dizzy, why his ears kept buzzing. It might even be why he kept forgetting things, because flu could really mess up your mind. When Jess was sick she'd seen a row of owls sitting on her windowsill, and when Mum had said there was nothing there, Jess had shouted out, 'But I can see their *feathers*!' Jess's flu had made her see things, his took stuff away.

He glanced back at the green cottage. Mr Whittaker had come out into the front yard and was raking up leaves from the lawn. He could get the old man to ring Mrs Mack;

she'd come and pick him up in her car, only he felt too tired to walk back down there. He wanted to go on sitting on this cool grassy bank a little longer, breathing the sweet spicy scents that drifted from the bush, watching the slow steady strokes of Mr Whittaker's rake across the lawn.

It was such a commonplace sight: an old man in a bright yellow sweater, raking up leaves, and yet it struck Clem suddenly as extraordinary, a sort of miracle. Why was that old man there—and the rake, and the leaves and the lawn—when in the rest of the universe, as far as you could see, there was nothing living: only howling winds and swirling gases, fire, rock and ice? And here on earth in this one tiny little place, there was a road among hills with a name of its own, tall trees with shining leaves, birds calling, a green cottage and an old man in a yellow sweater pushing a rake through the leaves? The sheer mystery of it brought an odd kind of comfort . . .

'Clem!'

He turned his head and saw Amy standing in the middle of the road. Clem leapt to his feet; this girl in the bright blue uniform terrified him now. A second ago the road had been empty, thick bush pressed to the verge on either side. There was nowhere she could have come from, in any natural way, not in that creaseless tunic, those unsnagged stockings and shiny shoes.

He forced himself to look at her face, and that nagging familiarity of her features clicked sharply into place. He knew who she was now: she was the girl in the old photo-graph Mum had shown them, the one who'd gone away to India with her family and never come back again. That girl had worn a tunic, and a hat, and her hair plaited in one long thick braid. 'Sweet Amy,' Mum had said, turning the page of the album. 'She was my best friend.'

Amy.

'Clem, come with me.' Amy held out her hand and he hid his behind his back quickly, like a little kid about to get a slap. He wasn't going anywhere with her and she wasn't touching him, even if he was right and she was the girl who'd once been Mum's best friend. Because what was she doing here, then, still young, no older than she'd been in that old photograph, still dressed in her school uniform?

Mum's Amy had died.

His eyes fixed on her lips; he was suddenly deeply afraid of what she might say next.

'There's something I need to tell you,' she'd whispered in the garden. He didn't want to hear what that thing was.

'Please,' begged Amy. 'Please, Clem.' Tears were running down her face. 'Oh, I'm so hopeless,' she sobbed. 'I don't know what to do.'

He felt no pity for her at all. 'Leave me alone!'

'Clem, listen to me, please. Your mum will get better if you go away. If you come with me—'

He hated her for saying that. She was mad. A mad, crazy ghost. That's what she was: a ghost.

'I've got to go.' He rapped the words out harshly. 'I can't come anywhere with you. I've got to get back to the house. I have to—I have to be with Mum.'

Forgetting his weakness, shoving it aside, Clem began to run. Halfway up the hill he stopped and looked back, knowing what he'd see. Amy wasn't there of course. In the front yard of the green cottage Mr Whittaker still calmly raked his leaves, but the road was empty where Amy had stood and the thick dark bush closed in on every side.

Chapter Twenty-seven

'Mum,' said Clem urgently. 'Mum, there's something I want to tell you.'

She was sitting propped up against a nest of pillows, her hair brushed to shininess and the ribbons on her nightdress neatly tied. The neatness sent a pang of sadness through him because he knew Mrs Mack would have done all that, while Mum sat still and quiet like a good little girl being dressed up by her nan. Her stillness never failed to stir up images of how she used to be: rushing in from school in the evenings, raving on about those kids while she took the clothes from the dryer, dragged out the ironing board, rushed round the kitchen getting stuff ready for tea.

Kids like Danny Hannan had been a grief to her, Clem could see it so easily now. Back home, where it might have mattered if he'd understood, he'd been as clueless as a five-year-old. He'd never seen the slightest sign that Mum had been heading for a breakdown—he hadn't looked, that was why.

The most shameful bit was how he couldn't even remember the day she'd got sick, how things had happened in the house.

Had Dad got a call from her school, or had Mum simply woken up that morning and refused to go, refused to get up any more? Had that day fallen into one of those holes in his memory, or had he simply been too full of himself back then to notice anything?

'Mum?'

She turned her head and her dark eyes, so like Vida's, fixed on him in that familiar baffled way.

'Mum,' he repeated, 'I want to tell you something.'

He sat down on the edge of her bed. Finding the right words wasn't going to be easy; he wasn't even sure he should be telling her stuff which would remind her of that school. He had to though, because he had this feeling he mightn't be around much longer—which was ridiculous, of course, and probably a symptom of this summer flu. But there it was anyway, this strange little kernel of cloudy knowledge in the very middle of his soul. The sense he'd soon be gone.

'Mum.' He took her hand, surprised by its warmth as he always was, because somehow you expected such a still silent person to be cold. 'Mum, it's about how I never used to listen to you, back home—you know, when you came in from school and started telling us about what happened there. And I should have listened, Mum, and I'm sorry, really sorry, I was such a stupid little nit. I was dead ignorant, Mum.'

She didn't smile. Looking into her eyes, if he hadn't known better, he'd have said she was scared of him. She couldn't be!

He squeezed her hand and went on quickly. 'The thing is, I honestly *didn't* understand. Oh, I know I'm seventeen and that's old enough to understand most things, but inside there's this bit that stays little . . .' So you're like a half-done cake, he thought, cooked on the outside, soggy and raw in the middle. Underdone.

He could remember being little, long before Vida was born, and how in the summer evenings Mum used to take him to the park in his stroller and give him a ride on the swings. Swooping up, wheeling out into the sky and then back down again, Mum waiting there to catch him, her hand on the back of the seat, keeping it steady while he flew back out into the sky again.

'Really little,' he said. 'Like when you used to take me down to the swings, remember?'

Her eyes flickered, so perhaps she did remember, and he went on, even more quickly now because it was so embarrassing, but he really needed to get it said, he needed her to know.

'And that bit of you which stays little, it makes you sort of dumb, so you can't figure out how someone who's an adult, who's your mum, could ever actually need you, see? How you could ever be any sort of help. It's no excuse, and I'm not trying to make it an excuse, I just want to say I'm sorry I was so dumb, all right?'

He wasn't sure she'd understood or even heard him, he simply couldn't tell, but at least he'd tried. Her hand slipped from his and twitched at the edge of the pillow behind her, as if she was tired of being propped up straight, made to sit up when she wanted to lie down and forget about them all. Carefully he slid the extra pillow from behind her back, plumped the other one and smoothed it beneath her head. Then he sat down again beside the bed. He felt weak and ill and even the comfortable old chair seemed to bruise his bones, but he sat on there till he knew she was asleep, holding her thin hand tightly in his own.

* * *

'Sorry,' Sarah's friend was saying. 'I'm sorry, Sarah.'

The weather had changed. It wasn't sunny in the upper quad today, but grey and gloomy and cold. Puddles of rainwater had gathered on the asphalt. Sarah and her friend huddled in the dry place under the stairs.

'I don't want to go, you know that,' said Amy. 'I don't want to go to India, but it's Mum and Dad, see? It's their job; if the church sends them, they've got to go. And me too. I'll write, I promise, I'll write every week, and you too.'

'Of course,' whispered Sarah, but then she cried, 'We promised we'd watch out for each other, always. All our lives.'

'We still can. It doesn't matter being far away. I'll send you an address when we get there, when I know. And it's only for a year.'

'A year?' It seemed so long.

'I'll come back. We'll be in fourth year together, you'll see.'

Chapter Twenty-eight

If someone is lying dangerously ill, a lighted candle
should be placed in a shoe and all other lights in the
room turned out. Then the name of the complaint
from which the person is suffering must be written
on a piece of paper and burned in the candle flame,
and at the same time the following rhyme should be
said three times.

> Go away death!
> Go away death!
> Life from the flame
> Give you new breath!

The candle must then be snuffed out with the fingers.

The Complete Book of Fortune

It was very late at night. Vida walked softly down the hall towards her mother's room. In one hand she carried a new brown school-shoe, in the other the candle she'd bought that morning.

Outside the door she knelt down and carefully fitted the candle into the shoe. Which way should it go? Which way should she turn the shoe? It didn't say in her book and Vida knew true direction could be important, like the way the front door of your house should always face the street. The front door of *Avalon* had faced the side, inviting misfortune in. They hadn't known the world was unsafe back then, they'd spilled the salt and crossed their knives and cut their nails on Sundays. And sure enough, misfortune had struck them down.

Vida turned the toe of the shoe towards the door, that must be right because the spell was for Mum. She struck a match and the candle lit first time, long flickering shadows dancing along the walls. From the pocket of her pyjama top she drew out the slip of paper where she'd written down what was wrong with Mum.

Vida had thought about that for ages because none of Dr Snow's words would do—trauma, shock, withdrawal— none of them were right for Mum.

LOSS, she'd written down at last, in big black capitals which almost filled the tiny page. Loss was what Mum was really suffering from.

Now she held the paper to the flame; the corner flared

brightly, turned grey, crumpled, and she began to chant her spell. Three times she had to say it, and she was just at the end of the second when she heard footsteps behind her and a small voice whispered urgently, 'What are you doing, Vee?'

Jess was hovering again.

'Vee?'

Vida clenched her teeth and ignored her. She had to concentrate; the paper was almost gone now, the small flames licking up towards her fingers. 'Life from the flame,' she whispered fiercely, 'Give you new breath.'

'Vee, watch out! You're burning your fingers!'

'Shut up, will you?' hissed Vida. Too late, because the door of Mum's room flew open and Dad stood there, his hair all tousled, sticking up in spikes.

'What's going on? Vida? What on earth are you doing there?' He stooped and blew the candle out. 'You'll burn the place down!'

Vida jumped to her feet. 'You've ruined it!' she shouted. It had to be snuffed out with your fingers, not blown out!

'Ruined what? What are you talking about?'

'There.' Vida kicked the shoe across the hall, it bounced against the wall, spilling the candle stump and bits of ashy paper on the floor. 'It won't work now!'

'What won't work?'

'My spell, for Mum, to make her better.'

'Oh, Vee.'

The sad exasperation in her father's voice made Vida want to cry. He didn't understand anything, he only believed in things he could *see*. Her voice rose up in a little kid's tragic wail. 'My finger's burned!' She held it out to him; she wasn't pretending, it did hurt, badly, as if all the pain inside her had somehow got in there.

Dad kissed it. 'Poor old finger,' he said in a voice he hadn't used since she was very small. 'Tell you what, let's all go down to the kitchen, eh? We'll get some ointment for that finger and Jess can make us all some Milo. You'll do that, won't you, Jessie?'

Jess nodded. It was like Vee was getting younger, she thought, going backwards, so Vida was the little sister and Jess was the big one now. Dumbly, she followed them down the stairs. Halfway down she stopped and looked through the window on the landing; she knew what would be outside there.

The garden was utterly still, the trees stood straight like soldiers and the ghost girl walked among them, up the slope towards that shimmery place at the top of the lawn.

When she reached it, the girl turned and stared back at the house. Jess still couldn't see her face, it was hidden by the wide brim of her hat, but she thought she could feel those goblin eyes upon her skin, the creeping touch of their hard cold jealous stare.

* * *

Somebody's crying, thought Sarah.

Was it Vida? She wasn't sure. She couldn't seem to wake up properly. She didn't know where she was. Sarah opened her eyes and saw that room which always frightened her, made her want to run away, backwards to that time when she and Amy had been friends.

She closed her eyes again, drifting, but now she couldn't get back, not properly. She wasn't in the upper quad now, she was at her own old house, her mum's house, standing near the empty letterbox while the postman's bike sailed on merrily down the street.

There was no letter from Amy. There hadn't been since Amy went away, not for ten whole months.

'Sarah! Sarah, love!' Sarah's sobbing had been so noisy that her mother had come running from the house. She folded Sarah into her arms. 'Listen, love, you've got to stop this, you're breaking your heart.'

'Something's happened to her! To Amy! Something bad!'

'You don't know that.'

'She promised she'd write. She promised me she'd send her address the minute she got there.'

'Sarah, India's a long way off, Amy's in a whole different world. When that happens sometimes you just lose touch; the people you knew in the other place, even your very best friends, they sort of—fade.'

'I wouldn't fade. Not for Amy. I wouldn't! Something's wrong!' Sarah gulped. 'She's got sick and died.'

'Oh, Sarah.'

'She'd remember me, otherwise,' cried Sarah. 'We promised. I promised, and she promised. Amy promised she'd watch out for me. All our lives.'

Chapter Twenty-nine

Down in the kitchen Jess stirred the milk in the sauce-pan. She watched the swirly ripples come, and the foam creeping slowly up the sides, and she felt it was strange that such ordinary stuff happened tonight—that the gas lit when she put a match to it, milk warmed and boiled, things worked as they'd always done, when the ghost girl waited outside.

She poured the milk carefully into the mugs and brought them to the table. Vida was sitting on Dad's lap. She was too big for it; her long arms and legs stuck out at awkward angles.

'I don't see what's so wrong with spells to make people better,' she was telling him. 'Nothing else works for Mum, does it? The hospitals, the medicines, Dr Snow. Why shouldn't a spell be just as good?'

'Vee, spells are superstitions. They were made up

by frightened people a very long time ago, they simply can't—'

Vida interrupted him. 'I know why nothing works,' she said hoarsely. 'It's because I have to say sorry first, that's why.'

'What?' asked Dad, but Vida didn't seem to hear him. She went on in that quick breathless voice which always sounded as if she was talking to herself, 'And I *can't*, see? I can't say sorry because there's no one to say sorry *to*. I can't get anyone to come.' She drew in a deep sobbing breath. 'There's no one there!'

'I'm here, Vee,' Dad said gently.

'It's not you I *want*!'

Jess saw her father's face quiver with hurt but his voice was quite steady when he asked, 'What do you have to say sorry for, Vee?'

'For what I did back *home*, that night when—' she paused to draw a deep quivery breath. 'You know, that night when Mum got sick. That was all my fault.'

'Of course it wasn't. You mustn't think that, Vee. What happened that night was no one's fault.'

'It was! It was mine. You don't know! I did something, Dad. It was something really little that you'd never even think about, but if I hadn't, we'd still be back there at *Avalon*, all of us, like we were before. It *was* my fault.'

Dad shook his head. His hand reached out to stroke her hair. Vida flinched away. 'Don't.'

Dad sighed. 'Okay then, tell me what you think you did that night.'

'I don't *think* I did it, I *did* do it!'

'But what? What did you do, Vee?'

'Promise you won't hate me.'

'Hate you? Of course I won't!'

She lifted her head and fixed her dark eyes on his. 'I turned off the TV,' she whispered. 'Before I should have.'

A silence filled the room. Jess didn't know what Vida meant, and she could see Dad didn't either. It sounded weird, so weird that for a moment their father looked almost frightened.

'But Vida, what could turning the TV off have to do with anything?'

'You don't understand!'

'Try me.'

'No!' Vida sprang up from his lap and stood before him, hands clenched at her sides. 'I tried! I tried telling you but you just won't understand!' She sank down on a chair, leaning her elbows on the table, her head clutched in her hands.

'Nothing's your fault, Vee. Please don't think like that.' Dad got up and stood beside her chair. 'Mum will get better, you'll see.'

He shouldn't have said that, thought Jess, and sure enough, Vida's head jerked up, those angry red blotches flaring on her cheeks.

'Don't keep on saying that!' she shouted. 'All right? Don't keep saying she'll get better when you don't even know, when nobody knows! And don't say that thing Dr Snow says, either. I hated it when he said that; I hated it more than anything!'

'What? What did he say?'

Vida's features twisted up in pain. She dropped her head and her voice was so low that Jess and her father had to strain to hear it.

'"Time heals all wounds," that's what he said.' A sob rose in Vida's throat and she said the words again so loudly they echoed from the walls like cruel blows. 'Time heals all wounds!'

Chapter Thirty

In his room at the end of the hall, Clem heard their voices faintly. Vida was shouting and then she was crying again, but he couldn't climb out of his heavy sleep for long enough to find out what was going on. And when he struggled awake at last, the house was quiet again. Whatever had been happening was over and everyone had gone back to bed.

Perhaps he'd dreamed the voices, because he felt damp and feverish as you did when you'd had a nightmare, and when he sat up, pushing the blanket aside, he found it hard to breathe. He could suck the air in all right but it felt like the wrong stuff inside his lungs, heavy and gluey, like stagnant water at the bottom of a pond. If he wasn't better in the morning he'd tell Mrs Mack about this flu, go to the doctor, get some antibiotics . . . .

His glance fell on the window and he saw it was closed,

the sheen of its glass went all the way down to the sill. Mrs Mack must have come in and shut it while he was out. That might be why he'd slept so heavily and felt so bad, so bad that crossing the small space between the bed and the window seemed to take an age.

The catch on the window took a long time, too. It was a different type from the ones they'd had back home; he couldn't figure out if it twisted to the left or right, and his fingers were so clumsy they might have belonged to someone else. He got it right at last, slid the pane across and looked up into the sky. The stars seemed even bigger tonight, huge and glorious—he'd never seen them so **close** before, even on those special starry nights out on the bay.

He glanced down into the garden, and his eyes widened with shock. It wasn't the garden any more. Outside there, angry and stormswept, rolling in towards the house, he saw a wild dark boiling sea. It had to be a dream, or fever, it *had* to be—but when he blinked and shook his head to clear the vision away, the sea still rolled and a great salty coldness rushed into the room.

The floor felt wet and slippery, tilting beneath his feet, and when he grabbed at the sill to steady himself, the window had gone and his frozen hands clutched at something cold and steely, the wrong shape. It felt like a kind of rail. The room sank away behind him, the sea poured in . . .

And then it was gone. The room shivered and grew solid again, he was kneeling on the floor beside the window, gripping the dry wooden sill, while outside the garden lay still and peaceful, all soft lawns and gentle trees.

He'd been seeing things of course, like Jess had seen those owls on her windowsill. She'd been so sure about those feathers, probably she'd even been able to smell them, just as he thought now he could smell the sea. He'd been hot before; now his teeth chattered and his very bones felt turned to ice. Summer flu, he thought. How could anything with the word 'summer' in it feel so very cold?

Chapter Thirty-one

Jess knew Vida sometimes went out at night. Often she'd been woken by her sister's soft footsteps and the faint click of the door. Vida's bed would be empty, and running to the window Jess would see her sister come out onto the terrace and stand there looking up into the sky.

Vida mustn't go out tonight. If she did, Jess knew the ghost girl would come down from her shimmery place at the top of the lawn. She'd hold out her hand, and this time Vida would see her, she'd take that hand and then she'd vanish, sucked away into the air. They'd never see her again.

Jess struggled to stay awake while the figures on the bedside clock rolled slowly over from one o'clock to two. At ten past two she fell asleep for a moment, waking with a sick lurch of panic, straining her eyes across the space between their beds. Vida still lay there, her dark hair spread out on the pillow— Or was that darkness a shadow? Jess sat up to get a closer look. No, Vida was there, still safe. Jess lay down again.

A quarter to three, three o'clock, ten past three . . . and at twenty past three Jess fell asleep properly. When she woke there was grey light at the big bare windows and everything in the room seemed to shout that Vida was gone: the empty bed, pyjamas and doona tumbled on the floor, the door half open on the empty hall.

Jess jumped out of bed and hurried through the house, past rooms she sensed were empty even before she looked inside. She moved quickly, yet her legs felt heavy and sullen as they had in that dream which now seemed long ago, and a coldness gathered inside her because she knew her search was useless: Vida wasn't in the house.

The front door stood open. Grabbing her jacket from the hook beside it, Jess ran outside.

The garden was full of mist and pearly light. A line of wet green footprints snaked up the lawn towards the place where she'd seen the ghost girl last night. Jess followed them, heart thudding, the thin soles of her slippers sliding on the dew-soaked grass. Halfway up the slope the footprints turned sharply away from the lawn, veering towards the drive. There were scuff marks in the spongy gravel, and in a muddy patch near the gate, the prints of Vida's boots.

The sun hadn't risen yet and the road looked different in the early morning, narrower and old; everything black and grey like the landscape in an old photograph. A small dark figure stood at the top of the hill. Jess caught her breath in a sharp little gasp of relief.

'Vee! Vee!'

Vida spun round. 'Go home!' she shouted. 'Stop following me!' She darted into a narrow track beside the road and was swallowed quickly by the close black trees.

Jess knew that track; they'd walked there with Dad one afternoon, through heavy bush and over pebbly gullies until the trees gave way and they'd come out on the ridge. They'd stood on a wide sloping rock with a great clear sky above them, shouting their names to hear them echo from the mountain on the other side.

'I like it here,' Vida had said. 'With that big sky and everything. It's the kind of place where you can think.' She'd looked up at the vast blue canopy above them— 'And where your thoughts might just get through.'

'I don't want you girls coming here on your own,' Dad had warned them.

'Why?'

'It isn't safe.' He'd frowned down at the long sheer drop to the valley below, and then at the rugged surface of the rock, pitted with cracks and small damp hollows where rainwater gathered and moss grew like bright green fur. 'You could slip.'

'I wouldn't,' Vida had retorted. 'I'd be careful.'

'All the same, I don't want you coming here on your

own, either of you. Promise?'

'Promise,' they'd said, but Vida's eyes had skittered away from Dad's.

It was dark in the bush when Jess reached the top of the hill and turned in along the track. White scarves of mist rose silently, drifting amongst the trees, and it was so very quiet that Jess stopped to listen. Shouldn't there be the sound of Vida's footsteps running on ahead? And birds— shouldn't there be birds?

'Everything else just slipped away, went still,' she remembered Evie Swann saying when they'd sat together on the bench outside the library. Everything went still when the ghost girl was nearby, as if her presence sucked all the sounds from the air. Jess looked round fearfully but all she saw was bush and mist rising.

'Spy!' a voice called suddenly, and the word seemed to clatter amongst the trees.

Jess jumped.

Vida stepped out from the place where she'd been hiding.

'Spy,' she said again. 'Why do you have to follow me everywhere?'

'I wasn't spying, Vee. I was only . . .'

'Only what?'

'Trying to help,' Jess finished feebly.

'Help,' sneered Vida. 'You never help me with anything!'

'Yes I do.' Jess bit her lip, thinking how she'd struggled

all night to keep awake so she could be sure no harm would come to Vida. Only she couldn't tell her that.

'You wouldn't help me with the planchette.'

'But that's—'

'Just silly rubbish.' Vida tossed her head. 'You don't have to say it, I know what you think!' She narrowed her eyes and gazed at her sister contemptuously. 'You're just like Mrs Mack, aren't you?'

'Mrs Mack?' Jess didn't know what she meant.

'Yes! You don't believe in anything, do you? Whatever you pretend. That's why you cry sometimes, in the night. Isn't it? Because you think when someone dies there's nothing—only bones and rotting and maggots crawling from their eyes, or—' Vida paused and added terribly, 'little *fish*, little fish nibbling at you, as . . . as they pass by.' She turned and rushed off along the track, swallowed in a moment by the mist and trees.

Jess stood absolutely still, her sister's words echoing inside her head. Why did Vida have to go and *say* that; say that awful thing about fish nibbling, when she knew how scared Jess was about drowning? Jess could see those fish so clearly: tiny little ones no bigger than darning needles, a whole bright shoal of them flashing through the water. And if there was someone drowned and lying on the bottom of the sea those fish would nudge at him, they'd nibble quietly, they wouldn't make a sound. It was so very bad to think about, so very, very bad.

Imagine a big white tablecloth, Dr Snow would tell her. And Jess tried; she pictured the cloth, she bundled it round the little fish and the sad drowned shape beneath the sea, and tried to toss it into the air. But there was nowhere to throw it properly with the dark bush crowding, and the trees shutting out the sky. Vida was right, you couldn't throw bad thoughts away.

A leaf spun slowly down from a branch above her head, falling coldly on her arm. Jess flicked it off and watched it flutter to the ground.

She looked round. She couldn't tell how long she'd been standing there, how long it was since Vida had run away and left her. The bush was silent again. Vida could have reached the ridge by now, so angry and upset she wouldn't be careful. She'd run out onto that slippery, sloping rock . . .

'Hurry!' cried a young clear voice that sounded very near. Jess's whole body jerked in fright. Along the track, a little way ahead of her, she saw a vivid flash of blue, a full skirt which swirled out for an instant and then vanished where Vida had vanished, into that same mist and trees.

'You leave her alone!' Jess shouted. 'You leave my sister alone!' And she began to run after the ghost girl, the blood singing in her ears, her feet in their thin slippers flying faster and faster over the crackly twigs and fallen leaves and sharp little pointed stones.

Chapter Thirty-two

Vida was alone. Jess saw that the moment she rushed out from the trees, the ghost girl wasn't there. But Vida wasn't safe; she was standing in the very place Dad had warned them not to go: on the rough slopey edge of the rock where it overhung the valley, nothing but sky above her and thick white mist below. The mist filled the valley like cottonwool packed tight between the mountains, so thick it seemed you could walk across it without falling through.

Vida was calling across the valley, her hands cupped at her mouth. 'Sorry! I'm sorry!' and the word echoed round between the mountains and rolled right back to her. *'Sorry, sorr-ee!'*

'Vee,' Jess spoke in a whisper, afraid to say the name out loud in case she startled Vida.

'Sorr-ee,' Vida called again. The echo seemed to mock

her, and it made her angry. She kicked at the rock, stamped and kicked again.

'Oh, don't,' whispered Jess. 'Don't, Vee.'

Vida stumbled, and then straightened. Jess heard her gasp. Then she stumbled again.

Time seemed to alter as Vida fell. It slowed, stretched out: Vida's hair flowed in a languid ripple, her legs folded gently, one arm seemed to linger a long time in the air. The two sounds of her name, when Jess called them, seemed to ring out for an age.

Vida was sliding towards the edge.

'Vee—' Jess caught her breath in a sob. There was too much space between them: the width of the track, a stony stretch of ground, the long slope of the rock itself— Jess knew she couldn't reach her sister in time. She tried though, she leapt forward—and then stopped in shock as the ghost girl walked out of the air and seized Vida by the arm.

She'd take her now, walk away with her over the edge— for a moment, the wild terror of it all made Jess close her eyes. She simply couldn't look. And when she *did* look, she could hardly believe what she saw.

Vida was safe. She was standing on the flat part of the rock, away from the edge, brushing the dirt from her knees.

Jess could tell from the way she did it, frowning a little, ducking her head to examine the scratches, that Vida didn't have the faintest idea how she'd been saved. She didn't see the ghost girl, she hadn't even felt that strong sure grasp on her arm.

The girl still stood beside her, smiling across at Jess.

Smiling.

Jess could see her face at last, and it wasn't the goblin face she'd imagined, twisted up with spite. It was an ordinary girl's face, a sweet face, young and kind. And there was something familiar about it too—not as a friend's face was familiar, or someone you knew well; more like a face you'd seen once in the newspaper or on the TV news.

Or in a photograph, thought Jess. Surely she'd once seen a photo of a girl who looked just like her. In Mum's album! That's where it had been: the old photograph of Mum and her best friend standing with their arms around each other's waists. 'Amy was the sweetest girl,' Jess remembered Mum saying, and then she'd added sadly, 'We promised we'd watch out for each other, for always—you know how you do when you're young.'

Amy. Amy, not Annie, her name had been.

Evie Swann had been right after all. Amy had meant no harm. She'd come to help them. Jess smiled shyly at her Mum's best friend, and with a little wave Amy stepped back, and the air closed over her so smoothly it was hard to believe she'd been there.

'What are you grinning at?' Vida was beside her now.

'Nothing.' Jess grabbed her sister's hand. 'Oh Vee, you nearly slipped over the edge, you nearly fell—'

'Of course I didn't,' Vida snapped. 'I was nowhere near the edge, nowhere. And don't you go blabbing to Dad. Or Mrs Mack.'

'I wasn't going to.'

'You'd better not.' But all at once Vida's bravado melted away and she let Jess hug her tight. 'I was trying to say sorry,' she whispered. 'I thought up here, with all this *sky*— I might somehow get through. But I didn't, it just kept coming back to me. Oh Jessie, I don't know what to do! And there's no one who can help me . . .'

She looked so miserable that Jess said at once, 'I'll help you, Vee.'

'You mean—'

'I'll help you with the planchette if you like.'

'Will you?' Vida's face lit up so vividly that Jess felt a queer little sense of guilt. She knew the planchette wouldn't bring back the person Vida wanted to say sorry to. You only had to think of the sure way Amy had walked through her doorway in the air to know real ghosts didn't need charms or spells.

'It mightn't work though, Vee,' she said. 'Even with me helping.'

But Vida only shook her head. 'We'll see,' was all she said.

Chapter Thirty-three

'That could be a C.' Vida leaned forward, frowning at the planchette's wobbly scrawl. 'Or the beginning of a C.'

It didn't look like a C to Jess. It didn't look like anything, and the planchette itself was tacky on their solid kitchen table, silly and flimsy, like those toys you got in Christmas stockings that broke on Boxing Day. The pencil wobbled and skittered over the paper, and the strange gleam that used to frighten her was only yellow varnish painted on so thickly you could see little bubbles in it, and tiny brush-strokes, too.

'Let's try again.' Vida took a fresh sheet of paper.

Shee-sha, shee-sha—the tiny wheels scurried, the same old loops and squiggles formed; curves that could be the sides, the tops, the ends or beginnings of any letter in the alphabet. They meant nothing, Jess thought, they never could, but the sea sound the little wheels made brought the drowning poem back into her head. She wished it wouldn't keep coming, she wished she could make it go away. *Full fathom five thy father lies; Of his bones are coral made . . .*

She knew someone who'd drowned. They all did. He'd been their very favourite person. They *never* talked about him, never said his name, though they thought about him in secret all the time. Mum thought about him, Jess felt sure, in that secret place where she was hiding from them. She'd got sick because she couldn't bear how he wasn't with them any more. None of them could bear it. When you woke up in the morning his absence was the first thing you realised, a dull slab of heaviness under the day.

He was the person Vida wanted to call back, the one she wanted to say sorry to, though Jess didn't understand why Vida felt she was to blame.

Her hand trembled and Vida hissed at once, 'You're not concentrating.'

'Yes I am.'

Vida took her hand from the board and leaned back in her chair. 'It's not your fault,' she said unexpectedly. 'It's this—' she glared at the planchette— 'this stupid thing!' and sweeping her hand across the table she sent it flying to the floor. The pencil snapped off with a little click and the board flipped over, its tiny wheels spinning in the air.

'I'm going to have to find another way,' Vida sighed.

What other way? wondered Jess. Another seance, somewhere else with people who mightn't be nice like Evie

Swann; people who tried to trick you, made their tables rap and float into the air? More dusty old books from second-hand shops, full of spells that didn't work and niggly little rules that stopped you doing anything in case it brought bad luck?

She pictured Vida standing in the playground of their new school, all by herself. She wouldn't make friends because her heart was so filled with a single wish that she didn't have space for other people any more. Katie's letters would go on lying on the table in the hall until Katie got sick of writing and found another best friend. Mum would go on lying in the room upstairs, and Dad would always be tired and worried and sad. Jess would keep waking up each morning with that same dull heaviness under the day.

Clem wouldn't have liked that, she thought. He'd be shocked to see how they went on.

'Time heals all wounds.' Jess understood why Vida hated Dr Snow for saying that. The person they loved wasn't a *wound*—a scabby old cut you wanted to heal up and go away so your skin was fresh and clean again and you forgot it was ever there.

They never talked about him. And they had to, she could see that now. They had to.

Jess took a deep breath. She didn't know what would happen when she said his name to Vee, but she was going to.

'Vee, it's been three months since . . .'

She faltered, stopped, overcome by the painful thoughts inside her head. 'Three months since Mum got sick'—that's what she and Vida always said. When what they really meant was, 'three months since Clem died.' Only they couldn't say it. They could barely believe it, even now.

But he *had* died. He'd drowned. He'd gone out in the *Sarah Jane* one night and been caught by a sudden violent storm. The *Sarah Jane* had smashed up, bits of the small boat had come floating in to shore, onto the bays and beaches and little hidden coves. Clem hadn't come back; they'd never found him. He was still down there beneath the water, in some secret place where the rips and tides had carried him. *Full fathom five thy brother lies . . .*

'Three months since?' Vida's frightened whisper broke in on Jess's thoughts. 'Three months since?' she said again. 'Since what? What were you going to say?'

'Since Clem died,' Jess answered firmly.

'Don't say that! Don't say it!'

'It's true, but. It's true, Vee.' Jess thought of Vida's spells and incantations, the seance, the flimsy planchette lying broken on the floor. 'And you can't keep trying to get him back, Vee. People can come back, but you can't make them.'

'But I have to say sorry to him. I *have* to.'

'*Why*? Why do you think it's your fault, Vee?'

'I told you. I turned the TV off.'

That sounded so crazy it frightened Jess, like it had frightened Dad the night before.

'But how could that make Clem—drown?' Jess found it hard to say that word. 'It was the storm, Vee, he got caught in the storm.'

Vida's eyes glittered. 'But that's it! That's exactly it, don't you see? It was because of me he went out in the storm! He was watching TV that night, it was the news. He was probably waiting for the weather forecast to come on, and I went in there—I went in there because I wanted him to help me with my stupid maths homework, and I turned the TV off, Jess, and then he didn't get to see the storm was coming!'

'But—but it wasn't on the weather forecast.'

'What?'

'That storm wasn't on the weather forecast, Vee. Don't you remember what the coastguard told Dad? How that storm was really sudden and no one had been expecting it? Not till the next day? "It came up too fast," that's what he said.'

'Did he?' Vida's voice trembled.

Jess nodded, thinking back to that night: the policewoman in the kitchen making tea, the man from the coastguards talking to Dad, Mum in the bedroom with Vida . . . 'You weren't there when he said it, you were in the other room with Mum—' Now Jess's voice was trembling too; she could hardly bear to think how Vida had been blaming herself all this time. 'You don't have to say sorry to him, Vee. And . . .'

'And *what?*'

'He wouldn't have blamed you anyway, even if that storm had been on the weather forecast, and he missed seeing it. Clem wasn't like that.'

'No, he wasn't,' said Vida softly.

'And you didn't know he used to take the boat out at night, none of us did.'

'I thought you'd all hate me!'

'Oh no! We wouldn't have!' Slowly, each word a painful lump in her throat, Jess added, 'Dying's no one's fault.'

'No,' said Vida. 'No, I guess it isn't.' They were silent for a moment, until Vida said suddenly, 'He would have loved it, wouldn't he? Sailing on the bay at night. He loved the sea at night, the stars—'

'Oh, yes.'

Did it make it any better if you died doing something you loved? wondered Jess. Perhaps it did, a little bit.

'Oh, Jessie.' Vida's next words leapt out in a rush. 'I keep hearing the telephone, the one at home, how it rang that night, you know? And then I hear Mum answering, her voice, and I see the curtains in my old room, how the wind blew them out, I can't stop seeing them—'

So that was why she hated curtains, thought Jess. That was why she'd ripped them down.

'I can't stop thinking about how it would be to drown,' she confided. 'Over and over, you know.'

Vida knew. They looked at each other.

'Bad thoughts,' said Jess. 'And you can't throw them away.'

'Huh!' Vida snorted. 'Dr Snow and his stupid white table-cloth!'

They almost laughed. Poor Dr Snow.

'I think he only wants to help us,' said Jess. 'He's nice, sort of.'

'Nice!' Vida snorted again, but she didn't sound so angry now. 'I'll tell you who was nice. *Clem* was nice. Clem.'

'Oh yes!'

'He was the best person. I loved the way—' Vida sniffed loudly, and went on— 'I loved the way he used to roll his eyes when he met us in the street, remember?'

'And how he'd say, "Hello, ladies!"'

'And bow to us, remember? Remember how he'd bow? And that song he used to sing, that one of Nan's . . .'

'Don't let the stars get in your eyes,' sang Jess softly, 'don't let the moon break your heart . . .'

'It's "steal", not "break",' corrected Vida. 'Don't let the moon *steal* your heart.'

'No it isn't, it's "break".'

'Steal.'

'Break.'

They grinned at each other. They were arguing in the way they used to, about something that wasn't really serious, and didn't hurt a bit. They hadn't done that for such a long time.

'All right,' said Vida generously. 'Have it your own way then.' And she went back to talking about Clem. 'Remember when he and Liam put that blond stuff in their hair and it turned green?'

'And wouldn't wash out—'

'For weeks!'

'And how he shut the roller door on Dad's car, right down on the bonnet, and Dad was in it!'

'Dad's face!'

'*His* face! Clem's face!'

It was wonderful to say his name again. They hadn't talked about him for months and now they couldn't seem to stop, and couldn't stop saying his name, over and over again.

Clem.

Clement David Sinclair.

Clem, Clem, Clem.

Chapter Thirty-four

In the passage outside the kitchen, Clem listened to his sisters talking and everything fell dumbly into place: the small cramped room full of dusty boxes, the single grey blanket on his bed, the gaps in his memory, the dizzy sickness he'd made himself believe was summer flu. No letters from Liam—people don't write letters to you when you're dead.

They don't speak to you either, or answer when you speak. Vida hadn't been angry with him, she'd ignored him because she couldn't see him, like the guy at the station who wouldn't sell him a ticket for the train. Mum was the only person who'd ever dreamed he was there, her puzzled eyes turning in his direction, speaking his name like a question. She'd known he shouldn't be here.

She'd begin to get better once he went away, Clem thought sadly. He'd hated Amy for saying that, he'd hated her because he'd known she was right. He'd known every-thing, and hidden that knowledge deep down in his mind.

Mum hadn't had the breakdown because of her work, that was simply part of the story he'd made up because he'd wanted so much to stay. Yet he was glad he'd told her how sorry he was for never listening to her when she'd been worrying about those kids at her school. He was almost sure she'd heard him, and he wanted her to remember him as someone who'd been trying to grow up a bit.

Slowly, he walked down the passage towards the front door. It was time to go. He didn't belong here any more. Out there in the garden Amy would be waiting for him. He'd been pretending about her too, until he couldn't any more, making up an ordinary world for her with a boarding school and parents who'd left her behind.

He opened the door on a brilliant night that brimmed with stars. Amy was sitting on the garden seat and she got up when she saw him, holding out her hand. He wasn't frightened of her now, he didn't hate her; she was Mum's old friend who'd come to help him leave.

He turned to look back at the house once more. The kitchen was in darkness, Jess and Vida had gone upstairs. Light shone from their bedroom and from Dad's study downstairs. The small night-light glimmered from Mum's room. The curtains were open there, and Clem saw a figure standing between them, gazing out into the garden.

It was Mum.

'Look! Mum's at the window,' he said to Amy.

She smiled. 'I know.'

'Can she see us?'

'I don't know. Only some people can. Your little sister sees me, but no one else does. Your mum sees you.'

Clem raised his hand in a small last wave, and Mum raised her hand, too. He wouldn't see her again. He wouldn't see any of them, ever.

Or would he? What did 'ever' mean? It was a word you said easily and you never really thought about how mysterious it was, and full of hope . . .

'They might forget me,' he whispered.

'No they won't.' Amy sounded so certain that Clem took her hand. He didn't get dizzy or sick this time; he felt exactly himself, the way he'd always be. He clasped her hand tighter and the great wide sky came closer, the stars rushed down to him.

Upstairs, Sarah turned slowly from the window.

She'd thought for a moment she'd seen Clem out there in the garden, but she knew she couldn't have. Clem was gone. The strange thing was how she'd thought Amy Atlee was standing beside him, holding his hand. Sarah smiled. She'd been seeing things, of course, dreaming—Amy had gone too, long ago. Yet the small dreamy vision had comforted her as much as if she'd really seen them both out there. She sighed, then lifted her chin and brushed her hair back behind her ears. It was time to go back to her family. 'We're here,' Vida's voice had cried out, piercing the safe place where Sarah had tried to hide. 'We're still here, Mum. Don't you even care?'

Of course she cared. Sarah left the room and walked out into the hall. Light shone at the end of it, and she guessed that would be Vida's room. Vida had always liked to stay up late. As she reached the door she heard voices from behind it; Jess was still up too. Vida's laugh rang out suddenly. That's good, thought Sarah, it's good she's laughing, and softly she opened the door.

They were sitting together on the red rug that had been in Jess's room at *Avalon*; crumpled envelopes and pages of letters lay scattered all round them. Even from a distance Sarah could recognise Katie's large uneven scrawl.

They looked up and saw her.

Sarah smiled at their astonished faces. 'It's only me,' she said. 'I'm here.'

Chapter Thirty-five

It was October 26, Clem's birthday, almost three years since
he died.

They'd brought flowers to the small cemetery on the
clifftop, to place on Clem's memorial stone. It was a very
plain stone, a soft grey colour with his name and dates
carved in gold.

They came here together every year on his birthday,
but there were many ordinary days when one of them,
Mum or Dad or Jess or Vida, might come separately and
sit there for half an hour, looking out at the sea.

'It's a beautiful place,' sighed Vida, looking back as Dad
closed the gate. 'Like a little island.'

'A green and pleasant land,' added her mother, as they
began to walk down the hill together.

Below them the streets of their old suburb glowed in the
sun's last light. They'd moved back to *Avalon* a year ago,

and Mum was teaching at her old school.

It was getting late, long shadows crept along the fore-shore, in the park little kids begged for one more swing before they went home for tea.

'Nearly summer,' sighed Vida happily. 'Nearly holidays.' She was a tall girl of seventeen, she'd be in Year Twelve next term, and Katie was still her very best friend.

Jess was thirteen and almost as tall as Vida; she wore her long hair in a single thick plait like her mother's friend used to do. Had she really seen Amy's ghost at the house on Hill-crest Road? Vida and her father said it was imagination, because they'd all been so unhappy back there. But Mum believed her, and next to Clem's memorial there was another stone, a white one. 'In Memory of Amy Atlee' it read, 'Best and Dearest Friend'.

The sea was very calm and still this evening: shee-sha, shee-sha—it didn't hurt Jess to hear it now. 'Don't let the stars get in your eyes, don't let the moon break your heart,' she sang, and nobody minded that she was singing Clem's song; they sang it together, walking through the park and along the familiar streets back home to *Avalon*.

ABOUT THE AUTHOR

Judith Clarke was born in Sydney and educated at the University of NSW and the Australian National University in Canberra. She has worked as a teacher and librarian, and in adult education in Victoria and NSW. She now lives in Melbourne with her husband.

Judith's novels include the popular *Al Capsella* series, *Friend of My Heart*, which was shortlisted in the 1995 Children's Book Council of Australia Book of the Year Awards for older readers, *Night Train*, Honour Book in the 1999 Australian Children's Book of the Year Awards for older readers, and *Wolf on the Fold*, Winner of the 2001 Australian Children's Book of the Year for older readers. Judith's books have also been published in the USA and Europe to high acclaim.